Band of
Acadians

Band of Acadians

a novel

John Skelton

DUNDURN PRESS
TORONTO

Editor: Michael Carroll
Designer: Jennifer Scott
Printer: Webcom

Library and Archives Canada Cataloguing in Publication

Skelton, John, 1942-
     Band of Acadians : a novel / by John Skelton.

ISBN 978-1-55488-040-9

     1. Acadians--Expulsion, 1755--Juvenile fiction. I. Title.

PS8637.K45B36 2009   jC813'.6   C2009-900500-X

1   2   3   4   5   13   12   11   10   09

We acknowledge the support of the **Canada Council for the Arts** and the **Ontario Arts Council**
for our publishing program. We also acknowledge the financial support of the **Government of Canada** through the **Book Publishing Industry Development Program** and **The Association for the
Export of Canadian Books**, and the **Government of Ontario** through the **Ontario Book Publish-
ers Tax Credit program**, and the **Ontario Media Development Corporation**.

Care has been taken to trace the ownership of copyright material used in this book. The author and
the publisher welcome any information enabling them to rectify any references or credits in sub-
sequent editions.

                                                        J. Kirk Howard, President

Printed and bound in Canada.
www.dundurn.com

Dundurn Press	Gazelle Book Services Limited	Dundurn Press
3 Church Street, Suite 500	White Cross Mills	2250 Military Road
Toronto, Ontario, Canada	High Town, Lancaster, England	Tonawanda, NY
M5E 1M2	LA1 4XS	U.S.A. 14150

Mixed Sources
Product group from well-managed
forests, controlled sources and
recycled wood or fiber
www.fsc.org Cert no. SW-COC-002358
© 1996 Forest Stewardship Council
FSC   98%

ANCIENT FOREST ™
FRIENDLY

For Brian and Hollyberry Oursie Bear with love

1

Grand Pré

Fenced-in yard of Saint-Charles-des-Mines Church, Sunset, September 9, 1755

"Courage, my dear, you must muster all of your courage," Nola's father said. "Your mother and I beg you to show your love by escaping Grand Pré this very night. Tomorrow will be too late. First thing in the morning the British soldiers will be shoving all men and boys onto those awful transport boats. That will be the end of our life here in lovely Acadia. We'll be landless and treated like dirt wherever we go. But you, Nola, with daring and luck, can get away to start a new life. We want you to escape to become our beacon of hope. Get away, dear daughter. Go to Louisbourg, or somewhere else that's safe."

"But, Papa, no! I want to help you and Mama here. I want us to stay together as a family."

"In a better world that would be the right thing to do, but we must accept that our life here is over. Be strong, my love. We've worked out a plan for you and fifty other girls and fifty boys to escape. You're a leader. We're depending on you to help lead those young people to a place where you can live free from these dreadful British soldiers."

"What about Mama? Will she stay with you?"

"Yes, we'll work together to survive as best we can. The plan is for you, as soon as it's dark, to help our friend, Hector, and the others to escape from this church that's become a prison. You and the girls must prepare hollows in the dikes by the west side of the Gaspereau River beforehand so the others have a place to hide from the soldiers. When the soldiers give up searching, the whole group is to scramble over to where our small fishing sloops are stored. Our hope is that those trusty shallops will carry you away from Grand Pré to a new life."

"Has Hector agreed to this? Is he ready?"

"Yes, Hector's very keen. He's sick to death of being shoved around by the military."

"Papa, if I do this, I may never see you or Mama again."

Her father hugged her tightly, tears welling up. "Don't despair, *ma petite fille*. We must hope that some-day, somewhere, we'll be reunited in a place that's safer than Grand Pré has become."

Unable to stifle her own sobs, Nola mustered all her strength and turned away from her distraught father. Looking up, she saw a surly sky forming — a south-easter was coming in. That could bring cover and a good wind for an escape. Perhaps she could make it all happen, after all. Slowly, optimism began to fill her as she contemplated the implications of the advancing storm. She walked nervously past the heavily guarded priest's house used as a headquarters by the British, and studiously avoiding eye contact with the soldiers, went straight to the spot in a field where her best friend, Joc-elyne, was picking corn. On reaching her friend, she whispered nervously, "Jocelyne, have you heard about the escape plan?"

"Yes, Nola, my mother told me. Our parents have come up with an excellent plan. It's scary, but I think we can do it. There are only three hundred soldiers here, and we're almost three thousand. It won't be easy. Those soldiers are tough, and they aren't playing games. Some of the meaner ones seem to enjoy harassing us."

"I know what you mean. Yesterday one of them tried to touch me, but I shrieked so loudly he ran off. It was lucky for me there were others around when that happened. It's going to be difficult and scary, but the more I think about it the more I believe escaping is the right thing to do." Hesitating for a moment, Nola continued. "Let's get a crew of girls together without attracting undue attention and start loading food in our shallops."

"Oh, I'm so glad you've agreed to come," Jocelyne said, reaching over and giving her friend a big hug. "I've got some corn here, and near our house there are apples, wheat, carrots, and turnips."

"That's my Jocelyne! If you could butcher a few dozen chickens, that would help, but you must do it quietly or don't do it at all. And try to get some blankets to protect us from the weather. There's not much time before Hector and company will be looking for our signals, so do what you can in the next few hours and then hide by the shallops. On second thought, I'd best get the rest of the girls and start digging hollows into the dikes myself. Are you going to be all right to get the supplies on your own?"

"I don't know, but I'll try. I know where everything is, including where the soldiers stowed our shallops. Count on me to do my best. But I'm not sure how you'll make those hiding holes."

"Try not to worry about that," Nola said. "You'll have more than enough to do yourself. Father told me how to work around the hollow places between the main supports in the dikes. We'll need shovels and saws for that. He said we need to make enough room to hide about fifty people. I think we can hide the entrances by replacing the flaps of grass. You go ahead and do what you have to do."

"Did you hear that your grandpa may be coming with us? The soldiers didn't lock him up at the church since it's so crowded and they figured he's too old to cause them much trouble."

"That's great news," Nola said. "He's a good man with lots of experience. I'm sure he'll be a big help even with that painful arthritis of his."

While Jocelyne busied herself with the food and shelter tasks, Nola moved on to some houses and scouted around for tools. Along the way she attempted to recruit a few girls she judged were responsible enough to handle the tough and dangerous job of tunnelling into the dikes. She found the tools she needed and convinced several trustworthy girls to take on the digging and sawing tasks.

About four hours after dusk the streets were deserted and dark enough that Nola felt the time was right for her and her crew to slink toward the embankments.

That risky manoeuvre went off without a hitch, and the dike work began. Nola was cheered that the wind and rain from the incoming southeaster helped muffle the noise of their burrowing.

Mud, restricted space, and dim lantern lights made digging and chopping difficult and sweaty, yet after an hour's work Nola paused to say, "You know, it's strange, but I find this work actually quite comforting."

Three hours into the task and bathed in sweat she judged they had made sufficient headway. She sat inside the biggest hollow, turned up the lantern, and called her fellow diggers. "Great work, girls, but that's all we have time to do. Give yourself a pat on the back. Our next step is for you join the others back at the shallops. There's no need to risk having all of you here when the soldiers chase after the boys. Anyway, there's not enough room. I'll stay behind to signal them. Go, run over to those boats."

There were many grumbles about leaving Nola alone, though everyone understood why that had to be. Those hesitating too long — and there were several — she shoved forcibly out the flap door, chiding them. "*Go!* It's the right thing to do now."

Shortly after the last girl slipped out, Nola climbed to the top of the dike and waved her signal light in a slow semicircle. She then crouched so that only her head and no light showed. Almost immediately shouts and thumping noises came from the direction of the church, and an instant after that a stream of figures rose out of the darkness and swept toward her at full speed. She doused the lantern and stood, casting a dim silhouette in the shadows of the night.

The first boy over the embankment hugged her, saying, "Am I ever glad to see you."

"Me, too," Nola said. "See the open grass flaps where we've dug holes? Wait there so the other boys can follow you in."

The boy whispered from the flap, "You've made a great hiding place, Nola." He waved to some other boys, and within a blink of an eye the whole crew crawled into the rough sanctuaries and pulled shut the earthen flaps. Except for the steady patter of rain, an eerie silence fell over the area.

Not two minutes later, they heard heavy footfalls over the dikes and then a voice. Hector, the only fugitive who understood English, heard: "I thought they came this way, but I don't see them anywhere."

"Keep looking!" said a booming male voice. "Those scalawags can't have gone far."

"Those youngsters are a bad lot," another, less forceful voice said. "Troublemakers — every one of them.

Someone planned all this, you can be sure. Only the boys ran off, while the men stayed behind to slow us down. It won't work, though. We'll get those little run-aways even if they do run fast. I'm surprised I can't see the rascals anywhere."

"Curse this rain, and no moon. It's too dark to see more than a few feet ahead."

"Look over there! Is that something moving?"

"Yes! Go catch those silly devils."

Fifteen minutes later the hideaways heard boots tromping again and the man with the booming saying, "It was a moose. I recognized those tracks. I think those accursed children have gotten away."

"Colonel Winslow won't be pleased we let them escape," the more timid man said, sighing.

"Only for now. We'll be back at first light to catch them for sure. They won't get far in this filthy weather. Let's return to headquarters. This rain is nasty."

Inside their dank refuge the fugitives crouched in silence, except for one boy who shook Hector and asked, "What were the soldiers saying?"

The youth's voice jolted fugitive hearts to beat in fear. Hector put a finger to his lips and shushed the boy with a vigorous shake of his head. Soon the patter of rain was again the only noise to be heard. After a nerve-wracking wait, with no new outside movement apparent, hope grew bit by bit that their pursuers might really have gone.

"I'm going outside to check," Hector whispered at last. Then a few moments later, from outside the flap, he said softly, "Everyone, come on up. It looks like they've gone."

The whole crew crawled out swiftly and clambered to the top of the embankment. Peering out, they spotted a dim light about a quarter-mile off in the church window. Although everyone was muddy and drenched, a cheerful mood filled the fugitives. It looked as if the first stage of their parents' daring escape plan had worked.

Immediately seizing the initiative, Hector asked, "Nola, where have the soldiers stored our shallops?"

"Across the river, about a mile along the shore."

Hector frowned. "We're soaked already. The river isn't too deep here, but it's possible this rain has already swollen its flow. We might have to swim a little near the middle. Don't forget to bring the tools Nola brought. Come on, let's get out of here."

Making sure the flaps were closed, Nola was the last to leave. There was no need to make it easy for the British soldiers to discover where they had hidden. Her home-spun woollen clothes were soaked through, her prized, lovingly decorated moccasins were coated with mud, and her brown hair was matted and tangled, but she was thrilled with their success so far.

Crossing to the east side of the swelling Gaspereau River, one of the smaller boys — only twelve years old — slipped and fell into the water. Struggling for air, he dropped the axe he was carrying.

Hector leaped into the river and easily pulled him to safety. "I hope you didn't swallow too much water back there, young man."

"Thanks, Hector. I'll be all right. Sorry about the axe."

"You're more important than the axe, my friend."

Eager to reach the shallops, the ragtag group skittered hurriedly along the shore. The lashing wind and rain limited talk to brief whispers. They all realized, though, that if the soldiers heard or saw them, they would be brutally hauled back and locked up. So few chose to say anything at all.

Only Nola knew exactly where the British had stowed their shallops, so she took the lead as they approached the storage area. Studying the site carefully, Nola recognized the shape of overturned boats emerging out of the darkness. She nudged Hector and pointed to them.

"I see them," he said, and sprinted over to them. As he ran, Jocelyne and the girls spotted him and left their hiding spot, waving and smiling with relief.

"Great to see you," Jocelyne whispered. "We hid the food and blankets in the bushes. The British patrol this area regularly. Unfortunately, they took all the oars and sails away."

"Hello, girls. Good work with the food and things. The missing oars and sails are a problem, though."

"I think I know what to do about that," Nola said. "I saw several British whaleboats riding at anchor earlier today — about a hundred yards back, I think. They might have oars and sails."

"Good idea," Hector said. "It's worth a try."

As the others helped to push the little sloops to the shore and load them, Hector, two other boys, and Nola pulled an empty shallop along the beach to the spot where Nola thought the whaleboats were anchored. They shoved off into the inky blackness, paddling hard with their hands and placing their fate entirely in Nola's recollection. Soon, just as Nola had hoped, silhouettes of whaleboats became visible. Pulling up to one, they all broke into broad smiles when they found it held not only oars and sails but a mast, as well.

Hector grabbed these and then untied the anchor line. "It'll drift off. No need to make it easy for our pursuers to get these back. They certainly aren't giving us any breaks."

They moved off to check the contents of another whaleboat. In less than half an hour they were rowing back to shore with a shallop full of equipment.

"We have all we need to set sail now," Hector told everybody. "The tide's ebbing and the wind's heading straight out of the bay — perfect conditions for us. Let's go."

They all hopped onto a boat helter-skelter, filling eighteen shallops with five or six persons per vessel. Most had a mixed crew. Hector, Jocelyne, Nola, and Nola's grandfather were in the same shallop.

Hector pulled up sail and pointed the tiller to head out of the basin. The southeast wind moved them along at a brisk speed. "At this rate by first light we'll be well out of here and deep into Chignecto Bay," he told them.

Ten minutes into the sail Nola pointed to several large sailing ships riding at anchor. "Those are the transport ships that are going to take our parents away to a very bleak future."

"I'm going to head away from them," Hector said. "We don't want any sentinels onboard to spot us. Signal the others to follow our lead."

All turned except for the helmsmen of two shallops. Seeing this reckless behaviour, Nola felt a shiver of fear. Instinctively, she reached into a food sack, grabbed a turnip, and heaved it with all her might at the irresponsible sailors. But her missile fell several feet short of its target.

Hector immediately scooped up another turnip, stood straight, and threw it as hard as he could. The vegetable struck the closest helmsman right in the chest. Both errant shallops began to turn away.

"Thank God that got their attention," Hector said. "Those fools would've ruined everything before we even got out of the harbour."

Pulling farther away from the huge ships, Hector managed a thin smile. "I cut more than fifteen of those whaleboats adrift. But the best part is that I found a spyglass in one of them. It's a beautiful piece of work. I just love it. The British are going to be mighty angry when they see what we've done. We'd better be far away when that happens."

"Nicely done, Hector," Nola said. She turned to her grandfather. "I'm so glad you could make it, Grandpa. Let me put this blanket around you. You look cold."

"Thanks, Nola, that does feel better. You youngsters are doing well so far, but you can be sure the soldiers will keep after us. When they notice the missing shallops and the whaleboats, it won't take them long to figure out what happened. They'll surely guess where we've gone. By sunrise, I think we should go ashore and hide the shallops."

Hector nodded. "Yes, we can't risk sailing during the day, but I think we can go until a couple of hours after dawn. I doubt the British will get far down the bay until later this morning. And the farther we can get from Grand Pré, the more difficult it will be for them to catch us."

As day dawned, a warm breeze propelled them along at a good pace, but a thick fog still limited visibility to a few yards. Nola was curled up under a seat, sleeping. Then she stirred, half awake, and grinned as she reflected on their new situation. They were much better off today than they had been last night. "Jocelyne" she whispered, "I need to go ashore. Do you?"

"Badly."

"Hector, Jocelyne and I need to go ashore. Could you pull in for a bit?"

"We'll go in for a quick break." He signalled with an oar to the other boats to head to shore. This time, to no one's surprise, there were no errant helmsmen.

Once on land, the girls managed a bit of privacy as they hurriedly completed their morning ablutions. Then Jocelyne broke out some cooked but cold bannock. Everyone ate the little snack with gusto; there were no complaints about the food being cold.

During the rest stop, Hector scolded the boys who had ignored his instructions. "We've got to stick together, or we'll all be captured. Next time pay attention. You could get us killed."

As their fellow escapees voiced agreement, the faces of the disobedient sailors reddened with shame.

Half an hour later, as they headed back out onto the water, Nola said to her grandfather, "You've been on the big bay before. How long do you think it will take for us to get to the isthmus?"

"It's almost seventy miles from Grand Pré across the Bay of Fundy to the head of Chignecto Bay. We'll have to be very careful when we get there. I heard the British have built a fort on the Chignecto Bay. They call it Fort Lawrence, I think. It's sure to be chock full of soldiers."

"Seventy miles," Hector repeated. "At our current speed, if we sail until about two hours after daybreak and then start sailing again three hours after dusk, we should get to the head of Chignecto Bay before dawn tomorrow. That will allow us enough time to hide ourselves and the shallops by first light."

"If this fog holds, perhaps we could light a fire to cook the chickens I brought," Jocelyne said. "The fog would hide the campfire smoke."

Luckily, it was still misty when Hector decided the little flotilla could go ashore again, so he agreed that Jocelyne could have a fire. In the high tension of arranging the escape, only Grandpa had had the foresight to bring the dry kindling needed to start a fire in damp conditions. Everyone was grateful for his good planning. The girls cooked breakfast, while the boys made sure the boats were hauled up and well hidden. Then they busied themselves erasing every trace of their passage along the shoreline. By the time the fog had burned off, breakfast was over, the campfire was doused, and all except two of their number were safely secreted deep in the woods, attempting to get some sleep. Hector posted the two exceptions as lookouts, with firm orders to stay awake. If patrols passed their hiding place, he wanted to know about it.

Although everyone was bone-tired, slumber didn't come easily. They were still soaked to the skin, and all were afraid of being discovered. It was only when they covered themselves with spruce boughs and endured much restlessness that they managed to get a fitful rest.

By nightfall, after all the worry of the previous night, everyone was relieved that no patrols had been spotted. "It looks as if we weren't followed," Nola said. "I guess the British are so busy loading our families onboard ships that they couldn't spare —"

"Get down!" Hector suddenly cried. "Take cover! Whaleboats coming!"

Everyone hunched down, sprinted back into the forest, and then lay flat on the ground, trying hard to make themselves invisible. Their concealment skills were about to be put to the supreme test. Nola hoped she had managed to hide all traces of their campfire, but she wasn't sure.

No one moved. No one said a word.

After a few minutes, they heard English voices as the whaleboats approached their hiding place. "It's getting pretty dark," one of the occupants of the first vessel said. "It's hard to spot runaways in this light. Maybe we should set up camp here for the night."

"No, we better head back," another man said. "Colonel Winslow will need our help to sort out the prisoners."

Shortly after this exchange, Hector peeked out and saw the boats turning around. "They're going back," he whispered.

They waited for a full hour, then Hector finally broke the silence. "I think it's safe now, but that was a close call. Let's move out. We have a long way to go before first light. Good thing there's another favourable breeze for tonight's sail."

Attempting to relieve the escapees' anxiety, Grandpa said, "This moist sea air is doing wonders for my arthritis. I should do this more often. My hands haven't felt this good in months."

"Grandpa," Nola said, "much as I sympathize with your arthritis, I don't think it's worth losing our land and homes for."

"Now, dear, indulge an old man. A little humour once in a while is good."

"Yes, Grandpa."

"Did you notice how everyone enjoyed our chicken breakfast?" Jocelyne asked. "That food was good for morale."

"Before this voyage is over, I expect we'll have some very lean times," Hector said. He glanced up at the sky. "The moon's out tonight, so we'll be more exposed. When we get closer to the head of Chignecto Bay, I'll go ashore and climb a tree to see if I can spot any campfires. It's great that I found that spyglass. If there's no fog, I expect I'll be able to see a campfire up to fifteen miles away."

The flotilla moved along some thirty miles without further incident until Hector decided it was time to check for campfires. He went ashore and climbed a tree, while the others stayed aboard their shallops, nervously waiting to hear what he discovered.

Calling down to the group, he reported, "There's a big campfire by what looks like a fort plus a few smaller fires close by. All the rest of the forest is dark. Those fires are about ten miles away. That's close enough. It's near dawn. We'll set up camp here."

At this second daytime camp everyone knew what to do. Again all traces of their passage were erased from the shoreline, and everyone tried to disguise the campsite itself. Unfortunately, there was no morning fog, so no fire could be lit.

Jocelyne arranged for a meal of cracked wheat, raw carrots, and some leftover chicken, all cold. When this proved to be too little, several boys went along the shore to hunt for shellfish. Hector insisted that they be back at camp within half an hour. It would be terribly dangerous for the band if any of the shellfish pickers was spotted.

"Better to go hungry than be a prisoner or dead," Hector said.

"We're making good progress," Grandpa added, "but it would be foolish to take unnecessary chances."

2

Crossing the Isthmus

Once they settled in, Grandpa informed his companions, "The isthmus is about twenty miles across at its narrowest, and we're about ten miles from the isthmus. I think that's too far for us to carry the shallops, particularly since we have to steer clear of the main trail to avoid British patrols. It's unfortunate, but we have to leave them behind."

"Maybe we can carry a few of them," Nola suggested. "There are a hundred of us. Surely, we could do that. It just doesn't seem right to leave them all here."

"It depends on the shape of the side trails," Hector said. "Remember, our priority is to get ourselves and our tools over to the other side. Once we get there, we can build rafts. Now let's get some sleep. We'll need to be alert and refreshed for the next stage of our journey."

"Yes," Grandpa agreed, "try to get some sleep."

Several hours later, as dusk descended, a crescent moon and light cloud cover spoiled their hope for complete darkness. But they all understood that staying where they were wasn't an option. "Moonlight or not, we have to press on," Hector told his companions.

After all the priority items were loaded in the shallops, it appeared they had enough manpower to take four boats on the crossing — ten people per vessel. Grandpa knew the trail best, so he took the lead, followed by Hector, Nola, and Jocelyne.

Three hours into the hike, with everything seemingly going according to their plan, Grandpa estimated they were well past the fort, which brought great relief to the refugees. Then, unexpectedly, three British soldiers bolted out of the forest and shouted, "Halt or we shoot!"

Everyone stopped, hearts pounding.

"Good!" the lead soldier barked. "Now hands up!" After a few of Nola's companions hesitated, he bellowed, *"Everyone!"*

Waving his musket, one of the soldiers said, "We were just out for an evening hunt and look at what we found — a bunch of wild runaways." Then, with a sinister expression, he pointed at Nola and Jocelyne. "You two, step over here. *Now!*"

Reluctantly, the girls obeyed this chilling command. Furtively, the soldiers whispered among themselves. It became apparent these were raw youths barely older than the fugitives themselves but scary nonetheless. After a few minutes, they stepped away brusquely and began pulling the girls into the dark forest. A horrified Hector acted without thought for his personal safety and tackled the soldiers. Two of the Englishmen fired their muskets, hitting Hector in the leg and another boy named Leo in the chest. The third soldier waved his musket menacingly as his partners quickly reloaded. "Back off or we'll shoot again."

Hector clutched his leg on the forest floor, and Grandpa cursed himself for not having sent scouts ahead. Nola and Jocelyne shrieked as their captors dragged them farther into the shadows. The soldiers and the girls were almost out of sight when, suddenly, a shot rang out and one of the English troops collapsed. Several boys, reacting on pure instinct, rushed to rescue Nola and Jocelyne, who struggled with their remaining captors. Assessing this new predicament, one of the soldiers panicked and dashed off. Just then a second shot rang out, and the fleeing man tumbled hard to the ground. Fiercely pummelling their final captor, the girls sensed their rescuers arrive and continued to wrestle the Englishman until he was flat on the ground.

Out of the woods came a large man dressed as an Acadian settler. "Good work, boys. Tie him up. I'll see if the other two are dead."

"Thank you, whoever you are," a shaken Nola said. She and Jocelyne hugged each other tightly. "Jocelyne and I owe you our lives."

"It's my duty to protect all settlers from dishonourable conduct," he said, bowing deeply. "My name's Noel Broussard, and I'm pleased I could be of service. I used to live nearby until the British burned down my house and imprisoned me and my family. I escaped, and now I wander around shooting as many Englishmen as I can. After what they did to me, I've vowed to fight for my family's freedom to the bitter end if need be."

Leo, the boy who had been shot in the chest, was dead. Hector had a big gash in his leg and had lost a lot of blood. Grimacing with pain but alert, he feigned good health but winced as he said, "Jocelyne ... Nola ... I'm glad you're safe. But we have to get moving right now. We're much too close to the fort, and someone might have heard the shooting. Mr. Broussard, thank you for your help. What should we do with that prisoner?"

"We'll take him with us. Let's bury your unfortunate friend and the two soldiers and get going. You're right, young man. It's much too dangerous to stay here."

To cover distance more quickly, the group used the main trail for the remainder of the night. Two boys, spelling each other every half-hour, held Hector so he could hop along the trail. His wound had to be patched several times to staunch blood loss. At dawn, when Grandpa felt they were more than two-thirds across the isthmus, they stopped and set up camp well off the trail. It had been a harrowing night, and all agreed it was best to rest and put off breakfast until dark.

Hours later, just as dusk was taking hold, the still-sleepy band heard a horse clopping through the woods. Presently, the rider, a tall, well-dressed teenager, appeared. Apprehensively, the stranger asked, "What's this? Who are you people?"

Broussard pointed his musket at the intruder. "A better question is — who are you, young man?"

"You're rebels! Agitators and scalawags — that's who you are! Well, we can't have that."

He turned his horse to leave, but Broussard stepped forward to intercede. "Step down from that animal, lad, or I'll shoot you."

The boy, his demeanour quickly changing from belligerence to dismay, slid off his mount, holding the reins shakily.

"We can't have you go back to the fort and reveal our position now, can we?" Broussard said. "To you we might be rebels, but we think of ourselves as people struggling to keep land we've owned and worked for over a hundred years."

Now thoroughly concerned, though still pugnacious, the boy spoke in a nervous jumble. "How is it that you have a British soldier as prisoner? What I see is that you're a bunch of rebels. My name's Frank, and when I was in Halifax last month, I saw your priest, Abbé Daubin, spouting all sorts of anti-British nonsense. I'm happy to say he was arrested and is in jail now."

"I'm sure you believe you're in the right," Broussard said. "But these boys and girls aren't guilty of any wrongdoing. Their priest might be, but not them. I ask you — what have these boys and girls done to deserve the brutal punishment meted out by your troops? They've lost their land, their way of life, and their parents. Anyway, we have a problem here, Mr. Frank. We can't let you go back. What do you want us to do with you?"

Frank mulled over his situation. After some hesitation, he reached a decision. "I'll tell you what. If you let me go, I'll take an oath not to reveal your position."

Broussard, Hector, and Grandpa considered Frank's offer, and after much deliberation concluded that the youth appeared to be trustworthy. No one wanted to shoot him. "We'll take your oath, lad," Broussard said. "But don't make us regret it."

Frank put up his right hand. "I, Frank Lawrence, of Portsmouth, England, do hereby swear not to disclose my contact with the group of Acadians I've encountered on the trail today, so help me God."

"Good enough," Broussard said. "You may go. Be worthy of our trust, young man."

"*No!*" shouted Nola. "We've suffered a horrible attack from this boy's soldiers. We can't let him go. That's crazy."

"I was bought up to be an honourable person," Frank said. "When I take an oath, I honour it till death."

Nola studied Frank skeptically. Then, gazing into his eyes, she noted his granite-hard conviction. Slowly, she felt her confidence in him grow. Perhaps he was someone who meant what he said. If he had been a soldier, she would never have believed him. "You understand that if you betray us, it would be a mortal sin?"

"I understand that, and I vow to keep my word. You can depend on my oath."

"That's exactly what we'll be doing if we let you go."

Frank and his horse were permitted to leave. He left behind a group deeply worried about whether they had made the correct judgment.

Jocelyne, her recent experience still fresh, opened several food packets with trembling fingers. A sombre Nola helped by handing out an apple to each person, including their prisoner. She prepared a pot of salted carrots, chopped turnips, cracked wheat, and leftover chicken. Because of their latest ordeal, they were afraid to light a fire, so they ate everything cold. That done they got back on the trail, fretting about what new dangers lay ahead.

Broussard had decided not join them. He would take their prisoner to what was left of his farm and have him repair his house. "I wish you all the best, but I have to go. I need to do everything I can to liberate my family. I hate to think of them suffering in jail. Remember, though, that the British are powerful, but if you're careful and smart, I believe you can succeed. Your parents are depending on you. Good luck."

Nola and Jocelyne were delighted to see the prisoner leave. Anger and relief flashing in her face, Nola said, "I hope Mr. Broussard works him hard. I find it difficult to forgive what he tried to do to us."

Jocelyne shivered and nodded. "I'm glad the other two were killed. It's awful that our Leo was slain, though."

Early that morning they reached the coast without further incident. Hector spotted many spruce and pine trees over thirty feet high and pointed to a grove with big trunks, indicating these would be ideal for building rafts. "Smaller logs would be dangerous if we get caught in a storm." Consulting with Grandpa, he chose which trees to cut and scoped out a trail to haul them to the shore.

The work proved exhausting. The girls hadn't brought saws or axes able to handle such outsized lumber, and the terrain was rough. Fortunately, they had managed to carry four shallops, so they would need fewer rafts. Grandpa estimated eight rafts twenty-by-twenty feet would be sufficient. Progress making these rafts was excruciatingly slow, however. Even with an all-out effort, a day later none was ready. Frustration mingled with deep fear seeped into everyone.

"This raft building is taking far too long," Nola said. "With all the noise we're making, at any moment a passing patrol might hear us, and that would be it for us. Maybe we should settle for smaller logs."

"It's too bad we weren't able to bring a horse or two to help us with this logging," Grandpa said. "We had over four hundred in Grand Pré. Sadly, they're all in British hands now."

Exasperation turned to full-scale fright when a suspicious figure stepped into their clearing. On closer inspection the newcomer proved to be Frank Lawrence, who was carrying a large pack.

Nola confronted him. "What are you doing back here? You haven't told the soldiers at the fort about us, have you?"

"No, I've honoured my oath, as I said I would. I'm here because I've decided to help you. The more I thought about it the more troubled I became by what's been done to you. The man who threatened to shoot me made sense. You're not rebels, and it's wrong to confiscate all your property, especially with no compensation. Our government should've offered innocent families land elsewhere. That would've been the right thing to do."

"Well, then, we're glad to see you," Hector said. "What do you have in that pack?"

"I figured you'd want to make rafts, so I brought some cutting tools and rope to tie logs together. I also brought some fishing gear."

Hector rummaged through the pack. "Perfect! That's just what we need. Now we can make real progress."

Still dubious, Nola asked, "Who are you? All you said before was that your name's Frank and that you come from England." She frowned. "And why do you speak French so well?"

"My Uncle Charles is the governor of Nova Scotia. I'm sorry to say that he's the man who gave the orders to have you deported and to plunder your property. I'm a student in England and I'm here just for the summer to 'broaden my horizons,' as my father puts it. I speak French because I spent many summers in Bordeaux where my family owns a vineyard."

Nola furrowed her brow. "I suppose that means you know how to read and write?"

"Yes, I can read and write in French and English, and I have a little Spanish, as well."

"Well, then, it would be nice if you could teach us. Our priest taught us to read a bit, but hardly at all, really. I hate that I don't know how."

"That isn't the way I expected to help, but I suppose I could do that."

"Great. Let me introduce you to the girls. I'm Nola. This is Jocelyne. Over there is Adele and Delphine." Nola followed with a long list of names. "I'll introduce you to the boys later when they take a break from raft building."

"It'll take me a while to remember all your names," Frank said. "I'm very pleased to meet you all."

"We'd better start using that fishing gear you brought," Jocelyne said. "There isn't much food for dinner, I'm afraid."

Several girls grabbed the new gear, hopped into the shallops, and headed off to catch dinner.

Much relieved at his good reception, Frank decided he would make some oars for the rafts. He doubted either his father or uncle would have approved of his new venture, even if he would certainly "broaden his horizons." Frank knew the long-standing tension between France and England would make his choice to help these fugitives a difficult one to explain to his friends, but he was determined not to stand by and do nothing. Still, he had to admit that taking risks appealed to him.

By mid-afternoon of the next day, they were all delighted to see the eight rafts completed. The sooner they left the isthmus the safer they would be. Hector decided the cod the girls had caught could be cooked ashore, but to speed their departure they would eat the meal itself onboard the rafts. So after the pot of delicious-smelling fish was ready, it was immediately transferred to the rafts, the fire was stamped out, and they were off.

3
Tatamagouche

Once out on the water, the ravenous crew consumed the fish stew.

"I've never seen a meal eaten with so much gusto in my life," Jocelyne said. "I guess all our hard work and relief at getting away made everyone extra hungry."

Although the sails on the rafts weren't efficient, they were definitely better than using oars alone. Hector said that should a raft begin to stray from the main group a towline would be extended from a shallop to tow them back.

It was a fitting reflection of the travellers' mood that a beautiful evening greeted the flotilla's first few hours back at sea. Several boys demonstrated their glee by diving into the frigid depths and splashing a few girls dangling their legs in the water — antics that sparked merriment all round. The cold water soon forced an end to this pleasant interlude, but the good cheer persisted.

Nola approached Frank after this little frolic to ask if he would convene their first language lesson. Noting there was nothing to write on, and concerned the dim light given off by their raft campfire would be insufficient for the task, Frank asked for suggestions. Grandpa overcame his wariness about taking lessons from this foreign youth and told him the Mi'kmaqs used the inside part of birch bark to draw messages. So, he suggested, since they had birch firewood on the raft, this technique might do. Several fugitives began to peel the bark from the birch logs. Such writing had to be done in two stages: they had to mark the bark with a knife, then fill these marks with ashes from the firepit. This method, though cumbersome, proved functional, especially after they piled a few more logs onto the fire to brighten the light.

Frank started the lesson by writing and pronouncing each letter of the alphabet in French and English and then asked everyone to repeat the letters and write them. After this exercise, he asked each student to write his or her name. Nola was absolutely thrilled when, in just over two hours, she succeeded in scrawling her name shakily.

"This is wonderful," she said. "I've wanted to write my name since I was a little girl. Father Daubin never taught us any of this. He mostly recited stories and songs from the Bible, which are certainly lovely. We had to learn many of them by heart. My favourite hymn is 'Ave Maris Stella.' It's beautiful, but I don't understand a word of it because it's in Latin. Now at last I am on my way to being able to write. Thank you for this amazing gift, Frank."

After the lesson, when the conversation turned to their travel itinerary, Grandpa said it was about fifty miles to Tatamagouche. At their current pace that meant they should reach that town in less than two days. They had enough water and firewood to last until then, so there would be no need to go ashore.

"That's good," Hector said, "because if we can stay five miles or so offshore, we're less likely to be discovered by patrols."

At about midnight three boys in the lead shallop — Remy, Joseph, and Pierre — spied several large seals basking in the water. They asked Hector if they could borrow the bayonets seized from the three soldiers during the isthmus fight.

"If we could tie a bayonet to a pole, we could hunt those seals," Remy said. "It would be good to catch one. We could use the hide to make shoes, blankets, and other things we need. And seal blubber can be used as lantern oil."

This argument convinced Hector, and he agreed to let them have the English weapons. "Just don't lose them," he cautioned.

The next morning several girls, who were shy about having so many boys about them all the time, decided they wanted to be on their own raft. "Some of those boys are entirely too curious about us," said one girl. "We need more privacy."

"Go ahead. Make the switch if you'll be more comfortable with that arrangement," Hector said.

They approached Tatamagouche near dusk in a good frame of mind until they got a closer look at the town.

"Oh, no!" cried Jocelyne. "Every building's been burnt to the ground, even the church."

"Over there," Nola said. "There are dozens of new mounds in that cemetery. At least they took the time to bury the dead."

Grandpa remarked that he had heard about some towns being ransacked before the expulsion at Grand Pré but hadn't believed it. "Now I see it was true."

Frank was shocked. "I've been told that war is

horrible. Now I see *horrible* in real life. Everything here is in total ruin."

Grandpa said that French soldiers were often no better. "The French were accused of burning the lovely Acadian border town of Beaubassin five years ago so the residents would have to move from English to French territory. That's the brutal reality of war. It's often a trigger for people to do cruel things."

Everyone strolled around the ruins, shaking their heads sadly and occasionally kicking a piece of charred wood. Hector, hobbling with a splint strapped to his injured leg, was the first to notice a trap door hidden under some burnt planks in one foundation. Apprehensive, he slowly opened the hatch and found a fair-sized basement. A beam of light revealed items that took Hector's breath away "Hey, everyone, look here! We're in luck. There are turnips, squash, carrots, and lots of onions down here."

After this discovery, the other youths looked more carefully, and before long the charred wreckage yielded more basement storerooms. Most had root vegetables, but one had several bags of wheat and oats.

Grandpa and Jocelyne wandered outside the town centre to see what was left in the surrounding cultivated fields. Most of the crops had been burnt to a crisp, but along one forest edge Grandpa spotted some unusual boxes untouched by fire. "Jocelyne, those are beehives, and it looks as if the bees have survived. Let's take them back to our raft. Once we find our own safe area, we can start a bee colony."

"That's wonderful! I love honey. And if we don't get those boxes, the bears will."

After his companions spent an hour hauling produce back to the rafts, Hector hopped up to the height of land above the ruined town. Surveying the horizon with his spyglass, he sucked in his breath — a patrol of more than twenty British troops was headed their way. Hector almost tumbled down the slope as he gestured feverishly to his friends and cried, "Soldiers are coming! Everyone get back to the rafts! They're less than a mile away!"

No matter how much they rowed and pushed, however, it soon became obvious that their slow-moving crafts would never get far enough to avoid being spotted by the British. Jumping off his raft into the shallow water and holding the three muskets they had seized during the isthmus fight, Hector said, "We've got to do something that will throw them off our trail. I need at least three fast runners to help me create a diversion. Remy, Joseph, Pierre, come with me. Wait,

I can't go with this leg of mine. You three will have to do it yourselves."

Hector handed Remy, Joseph, and Pierre each a firearm. Without hesitating, Frank leaped into the water. "I'm going, too. The more we are the better chance we have to get those soldiers to chase us."

Hector nodded. "We'll get offshore as quickly as we can and then head east. At dawn we'll come back to look for you. With luck you'll have led the soldiers away and be waiting for us. Good luck!"

Nola, Hector, and the others onboard watched anxiously as the four scurried up the slope. As soon as they were out of sight, three shots rang out. Five minutes later another three were followed by a continuous fusillade. After the last barrage, faint shouts were heard and then silence.

An hour later the runaways were almost a mile offshore and still hadn't glimpsed any soldiers on the hill nor heard more shots. "It's dark," Nola said. "We'll be completely out of view in a few more minutes. We might be safe, but I don't know about our brave boys. I pray they get away."

"Yes," Grandpa said. "Let's pray for them." Everyone on Grandpa's raft knelt and recited a prayer taught to them by Father Daubin:

"O most powerful and glorious Lord
God who rules and commands all things,
stir up thy strength and save our boys
from their enemies. Hear thy poor ser-
vants pleading for thy help and defend
our friends against their enemies. Amen."

Shortly after the flotilla cleared the horizon, a sud-
den squall nearly swamped the group. The choppy water
and fear for the diversion crew's fate sapped everyone's
appetite. A few munched gloomily on carrots, while others chewed raw oats just to while away the time. No one
dared to light a fire — it would have drawn too much
attention to their position.

At the first hint of dawn, still encircled in dangerous
whitecaps, they turned toward shore. Everyone strained
their eyes for signs of the diversion crew, but there was
no trace of the four boys. By noon, despondency took
hold of them. The valiant squad must have been either
taken prisoner or killed. With sorrow Grandpa suggested they again kneel in prayer.

They were just settling onto their knees when Jocelyne looked up. "I see them!" She pointed at a large
rock in the distance where four shadowy figures waved
enthusiastically. Everyone shouted with glee. Those in

the shallops started rowing furiously toward the rock.

Nola blinked. "I don't see them. Everyone's eyesight must be better than mine."

As they drew nearer to the rafts, a raucous cheer boomed across the water to greet the brave boys. When the boys finally got onboard, they were met with hugs and smiles of relief.

"We were beginning to think you were dead," Hector said.

"It was close," a haggard Remy said. "Once they spotted us those soldiers kept after us for miles. They didn't give up easily. It was the thick forest, our fast pace, and the dark that finally won the day for us."

"We prayed for you," Nola said. "I think that helped, too."

4
To St. Peter's

Jocelyne led a group of girls in the preparation of a feast for the returning heroes. In the hours since leaving Tatamagouche, their fishing lines had hooked several cod, and these became the main dish to a meal that included wheat cakes fried in cod oil and a selection of the choicest vegetables found in the ruined town.

Frank enjoyed the meal immensely. "Jocelyne, I've eaten at fancy banquets in some of the most elegant homes in England and France, but your dinner tops them all. You're an amazing cook."

"Thank you, Frank, but I had a lot of help. And it's hard to go wrong when you're frying freshly caught cod."

During the meal, Pierre recounted an incident that had occurred in the course of the boys' diversion. "After we fired our muskets for the second time, we ran to a heavily forested valley about three miles south of the town. We were surprised when we came across a group of oddly dressed men from Grand Pré. I recognized several of them. They were the ones the British were really after, not us. They escaped from the transport ships by disguising themselves in women's clothing. The guards allowed women to bring food to the prisoners but hadn't bargained they'd hide women's dresses in the food baskets. The fugitives told us, though, that they had decided to give themselves up. They said they couldn't bear to leave their wives behind."

In between mouthfuls of a wheat cake, Hector asked, "Did they say anything about what happened after our escape was discovered?"

"Oh, yes! The morning the soldiers discovered the missing whaleboats and shallops they said Colonel Winslow turned beet-red with rage. He ordered a whole platoon to search for us, but a day later they came back empty-handed and dejected."

Hector roared with laughter. "It feels good to give those soldiers a taste of their own medicine. Maybe now they'll have an idea how unhappy we 'scalawags' are to see our property plundered."

Nola was so overcome with joy suddenly that she went over to Hector and gingerly planted a kiss on his forehead. Still laughing, he glanced up in surprise. "You're a hero, too, Hector. Your injury might have stopped you from joining the diversion crew, but you and Mr. Broussard saved Jocelyne and me back at the isthmus. That was a brave thing to do. Thank you."

"As Mr. Broussard said, it was my pleasure, Nola. My leg's getting better now. This splint's helping a lot."

Jocelyne hurried over to Nola and gestured that she should join her at a spot behind some firewood where Hector couldn't see them. Once behind this cover, Jocelyne whispered, "Nola, I thought you were my friend. Why did you kiss Hector like that?"

"What do you mean?"

"I hope you're not trying to make Hector sweet on you."

"I was just saying thank you, Jocelyne. You can do the same thing if you want."

"I will not! You're causing trouble when you kiss him. I sincerely hope you won't do that ever again."

Nola was surprised at her friend's fury. She didn't

know what to say, so she turned away and started cleaning up the remains of the celebratory meal.

Adele, one of the more gregarious girls, approached Nola. "I'm no longer happy being on a girl-only raft. It's true some of the boys are rude and rough — that's why we moved three days ago — but those boys are also fun and I want to go back. Being shy is boring."

"There certainly isn't much privacy on these rafts," Nola said. "But there's nothing to stop you from going. There's no need to be shy. Just ask one of the boys in a shallop to row you over."

"Good. Then that's what I'll do." She giggled. "I think I know how to teach the rougher boys some manners."

Nola smiled and continued working.

A little later Hector asked Grandpa the distance to the Strait of Canso.

"It's about a hundred and fifty miles from Tatamagouche to St. Peter's," Grandpa said. "At St. Peter's there's a haul-over road for boats to get into the Bras d'Ors."

"Why would we want to go to the Bras d'Ors? Isn't the shorter way to Louisbourg to follow the coast?"

"Yes, but it can get very rough out in the open ocean, especially as winter approaches. Our rafts would never hold together if we got caught in an ocean storm. The

Bras d'Ors is still salt water, and though it's a longer route, it's a lot safer."

"That makes sense. To reach St. Peter's will take us about seven days. I don't want to risk going ashore again, but we might have to if we run short of firewood or drinking water. I'll tell everyone to keep a tight rein on their use of our supplies."

Jocelyne ambled over to Grandpa and asked him how she should take care of the beehives.

"The bees will go into hibernation when you cover up the hive," he told her. "They'll survive to the spring as long as they're protected from freezing. When the outside air temperature decreases, the bees cling tightly together in clusters on the combs so the larger clusters have a better chance for survival than the smaller ones. Honeybees can't survive a hard frost, so we have to help them keep warm by covering the hive with moss or some other insulation."

"Thanks, Grandpa. I'll do that."

Frank was standing nearby and had overheard their conversation. "That reminds me of the problems taking care of another little creature important to humans — silkworms. I've heard there are quite a few silk cultivators in France who lost their little creatures to cold temperatures. The silkworm is as tiny as a bee, but when thousands are feeding, the grinding noise of their jaws is so loud it sounds like heavy rain striking leaves during a thunderstorm. I found it amazing that such a little creature could make such a big noise."

Paying no attention to his comments about silkworms, Nola asked Frank, "Are you recovered enough from your adventure to give us another writing lesson?"

"Sure." Then he looked at some of the other girls. "Everyone interested in writing lessons go get your writing barks and charcoal pencils." Ten minutes later he started the lesson. He reviewed the alphabet and had his students spell out a few everyday words. After an hour of that, he introduced numbers and even had a few of the faster learners do simple arithmetic.

When the students had all worked hard for three hours, shouts from the lead shallop were heard and they took a break to see what the commotion was about. Remy and Joseph had surprised a basking seal and were busily spearing it with their bayonet-tipped poles. The animal soon succumbed to their vigorous thrusts, and the carcass was hauled aboard the nearest raft. The ensuing butchering was gory, upsetting even the stoutest hearts, but the result would produce much-needed sealskin and blubber. Even without being tanned and still greasy, the sealskin could be put to use as waterproof blankets and the blubber as heating oil. Few were interested in eating the gamy meat, so it was thrown into the water, which proved to be a huge mistake.

A migrating walrus, apparently very hungry, approached the raft to feed on the huge gobs of seal meat. Not considering the consequences of enraging such a powerful beast, Joseph speared it. The wounded giant bellowed with rage and charged the raft, its massive tusks snapping at the logs and brutally throwing three boys high into the air. Flailing in the water, these three struggled desperately and barely managed to get back onboard.

As he pulled up Joseph, Hector said, "Spearing that beast was a foolish thing to do."

"I ... I never thought it would attack us. I ... I'm glad no one was hurt."

"And I'm glad it's gone," Grandpa added. "Walruses usually eat things like octopus and shellfish. It must have been all the seal blood and gore that attracted it."

The excitement of the seal hunt and rescue from the angry walrus boosted most of the crew's morale, but not Adele's. She came over to Nola with a new complaint. Like others in the dike-digger group at Grand Pré, she hadn't had the opportunity to bring personal care items such as hairbrushes. The supply girls, however, were able to take whatever they needed. Adele missed her hairbrush, particularly now that she was on a mixed-gender raft. "It's not fair that the supply girls are better groomed than we are," she told Nola.

Nola called over Delphine, one of the supply girls. "Would you help Adele and I make some soap, Delphine? With the seal blubber and wood ash, we can make lye soap."

"Sure. That sounds like fun."

In less than two hours they produced their first batch. That done, Nola said, "Let's test it on your hairbrush, Delphine. I think it'll do a good job of cleaning the brush."

After they washed the brush, Delphine said, "It's certainly cleaner."

Nola smiled. "Good. Would you lend your brush to Adele if she agrees to wash it after she uses it?"

"I guess I could do that."

"Now, girls, I have another suggestion. You know how Grandpa complains about his sore teeth? Well, if you use a toothpick after every meal, discreetly, of course, and then swish out your mouth with this lye soap, you'll not only have fresher mouths but you'll have healthier teeth. It won't taste good, but you can chew some spruce gum to get rid of the bad taste. How would you like that?"

Adele grimaced. "The soap bit sounds nasty, but I'll try it."

Delphine also agreed. Shortly afterward, Nola was delighted to see the two girls go hand in hand to the raft shelter, presumably, she thought, to try out their new hygiene routine.

Seven days after leaving Tatamagouche, the flotilla entered Canso Strait. "It looks like another southeaster is coming in," Hector said. "If we can reach St. Peter's by tomorrow, that would be good. We don't want to get caught in the strait when the storm hits. An ocean storm can be brutal."

The next morning, as the big storm approached, they sailed into the safety of St. Peter's Bay. They had to row the last dozen yards, though, before were able to step ashore.

"Whew!" Jocelyne said. "The firm ground certainly feels wonderful after so many days of bouncing up and down in rough water."

Exploring their landing site, Hector discovered that it took only ten minutes to walk over the haul-over road to reach the salt water of Bras d'Ors. "We might have to take apart the rafts to get them over the road, but even if we have to do that, it won't be that terrible. It'll give us time to repair the raft attacked by the walrus. I'm going to ask our three best shooters to go out and shoot us a deer right now. As long as we can hide the rafts and shallops partway up the trail, we can finish that transport job tomorrow. We're due for another celebration. We're back on French territory!"

Wind and rain beat down on the group as they dragged the rafts up the slope. But no complaints were voiced — the rain-created mud made their sliding job easier if more messy. As for the three hunters, the storm was also more of a plus than a drawback; it muted the sounds made as they crept up to a big buck. By late afternoon, they made the kill. Although everyone was tired, preparations for a nighttime feast began in earnest — this happy occasion wasn't a time for sleep.

A few boys built a lean-to shelter for the fire, and this cover was soon extended to protect a larger area. Before long the aroma of roast venison permeated the moist nighttime air. Hector whittled a fresh pine branch with a soft centre into a whistle. This proved less than satisfactory, so he took a deer leg bone, dug out the marrow, and punched a few holes into it. Soon the melodies of a flute drifted across the campsite.

Other would-be musicians followed Hector's lead and crafted all kinds of deer bones into flutes of surprising variety. They also made music from whatever else was available, including tapping spoon-shaped wooden sticks. As for the feast, venison proved to be not only the main course but almost the only course. They had run out of vegetables except for a few turnips. The feasting and frolicking went on until the wee hours of the morning.

Late the next day the fugitives' guard went over to Hector and nudged him awake. "We have visitors."

Hector pulled himself up and blinked sleepily at the older man and woman above him. "Hello, hello! I hope you don't mind us camping here. We're refugees from Grand Pré."

"You're most welcome," the older man said. He identified himself as Monsieur Denys, and his wife as Madame Denys. They were the guardians of the haul-over road. The couple had seen the campfire and heard sounds the night before but had been unsure about their own safety, so they had decided to wait until morning to investigate. "We heard you partying last night. It seems like you didn't let the rain stop you from having a good time."

"Yes, we had fun. Some of us can actually carry a tune." As was the custom of their people, Hector wanted to offer the visitors food but was unable to do so. "I'm sorry I can't offer you anything to eat. We ate everything last night."

"That's quite all right. Come over to our cottage when you're rested and we'll be pleased to make you tea."

"Thank you," Hector said. "You're very kind to offer us hospitality after we kept you awake." Hector decided to follow the couple right away. While he walked beside the couple, he noticed that Monsieur Denys was at least as old as Grandpa but appeared to tire more easily.

When Hector told them about their adventures, especially how his leg had been wounded, Madame Denys said, "You're a brave young man. Your injury is a badge of courage. I'm going to give you some of my very best 'special occasion' cookies with your tea. Everything in the cookies comes from our garden."

Two hours later Hector returned to their campsite weighed down with a bag full of vegetables, including potatoes and tomatoes, which he had heard about but had never seen before. Monsieur and Madame Denys had told him that the seeds for these crops had come from the Mi'kmaq, who had traded for them with another Native tribe far to the south.

Nola and Jocelyne were excited to see, and taste, the new foods and agreed they would be excellent additions to their cuisine. Curious about Monsieur and Madame Denys and wanting to thank them for their generosity, the girls strolled over to the couple's cottage.

"Hello, Madame Denys," Nola said when they arrived. "We ate some of the potatoes and tomatoes you gave Hector and wondered if you'd show us those plants."

"Of course! I love to show off my garden, particularly to young ladies who appreciate its value. There are some plants I didn't give to Hector that you might like to see. For example, look at this tobacco leaf." She pointed at a tall, big-leafed plant. "It's much loved by the Mi'kmaq people. The soil in this meadow is rich, and the area is well sheltered from cool ocean breezes. Unfortunately, the growing season is too short to support many grain crops, so we have to buy those from farmers farther south."

"It must be fun to make a meal when you have so many wonderful ingredients," Jocelyne said.

"That gives me an idea," Madame Denys said. "If you two will help, I'll prepare a nice dinner for, say, twelve of you. That's all we have room for in this cottage. Make sure that young man with the leg splint, the English lad, and the older man are among those you invite."

"Thank you, Madame Denys," Nola said. "We'll go back to our camp and make arrangements. You're very kind."

The cottage dinner was set for the next evening. Hector decided to choose the seven other invitees via a long-stick, short-stick lottery. Those not invited were allowed to shoot another deer and get vegetables from Madame Denys's garden to fashion their own meal.

The day of the dinner Jocelyne and Nola went over to the cottage in the early afternoon, keen to help Madame Denys with meal preparations. All was ready when the remainder of the dinner group arrived just as the sun was setting. Monsieur and Madame Denys greeted each guest with much ado and a cheery "Welcome! Welcome!"

Everyone was in good spirits until dessert was served. Madame Denys then turned the mood sombre. "Much as my husband and I would like you to stay, this isn't a safe place for you. Several of the French officers stationed at Louisbourg are cruel to homeless people like you. They often drop by St. Peter's and might decide to force you to work without paying you a penny. The Denys family used to be fairly rich from exporting wood, fish, and furs to France, but unscrupulous deals by the governor have ruined our business. Laws are passed just for the benefit of the ruling class. Ordinary people have no say. It's an unfair system. I remember —"

"Madame exaggerates a little," Monsieur Denys cut in. "Our three sons were press-ganged into the military four years ago, and it's quite likely we'll never see them again. This has crushed our spirit. Louisbourg is actually doing quite well at present. The population is growing, and the fishery is earning huge revenues for the French crown. Settlers have a higher standard of living than commoners do in France. But all this is fragile. Crises of various sorts, such as the sinking of a supply ship or war, often cause the governor to trample on people's rights. When such things happen, ordinary people have no recourse. The system protects only the ruling class."

Nola frowned. "Where should we go then?"

"There's no really safe place," Madame Denys said, "but if you go to Whycocomagh, the Mi'kmaq will help you as long as you respect their land and traditions. They're a mild and peaceful people who we've come to like and respect."

Monsieur Denys stood and asked Hector to do the same. "We have a gift for you. I've drawn a map of the Bras d'Ors area, showing the settlements and areas of interest. Over many years the Denys family has explored and mapped the whole of the island, identifying the location of coal seams, limestone and gypsum deposits, and an area around Baie des Espanols where there's an extrusion of red rock we believe is some sort of mineral."

"Thank you very much, Monsieur Denys. This map is hugely valuable. It'll help us find our way in this new land."

Madame Denys stood and asked Frank to stand. "I understand you're the young man who gives writing lessons. As our children were growing up, we read them stories from this lovely book by Charles Perrault. It includes the fairy tales "Little Red Riding Hood," "Sleeping Beauty," "Puss in Boots," "Cinderella," and "Bluebeard." They're wonderful tales that stir the imagination of young and old. We want you to have this book." With a hug and a big smile, Madame Denys handed the volume to Frank.

Frank leafed through the book, marvelling at its wonderful illustrations. Then he turned to the frontispiece and saw that Madame Denys had written a dedication. He read it aloud:

> "To *les rameurs*. May this book bring you
> as much joy as it brought to our family.
> Monsieur and Madame Paul Denys
> October 1755"

"Les Rameurs!" Frank cried. "The Oarsmen! We were wondering what we should call ourselves. That's a great name."

Murmurs of approval spread around the table, with much nodding and repeatings of *"Les Rameurs!"*

"You youngsters have raised our spirits and given us hope for the future," Madame Denys said, tears in her eyes. "We wish you every success on your voyage."

The next day Nola said to Hector, "We're ready to go except Grandpa and two boys who are still out hunting. Grandpa says he needs more time to steep the deer and sealskin hides in warm water and oak bark or the tanning won't be right. But those boys should have been back hours ago."

"I'll help him bring the tanning pot onboard one of our rafts," Hector said. "Those boys, however, are truly irresponsible. With the cold weather coming we can't be dallying."

Two hours later the boys returned, holding a couple of rabbits they had shot. They were quite pleased with themselves.

Hector brusquely changed their mood. "If you're expecting praise for shooting those rabbits, forget it. You were told to be back at camp before noon. We've been delayed because of your thoughtlessness. I'm taking those muskets back. Only responsible boys get issued guns."

The eight rafts and four shallops at last headed out to sea. Monsieur and Madame Denys waved a tearful goodbye and shouted, *"Bon voyage les rameurs!"*

As they pulled out, Nola said to Frank, "You must be pleased we aren't going to Louisbourg. I don't think an Englishman would get a very good reception there. Whycocomagh sounds better to me, too. I'm looking forward to meeting the Mi'kmaq."

Frank grinned. "I'm starting to believe it can be dangerous to go anywhere today. As for the Mi'kmaq, it'll be important to get along with them. They might not be happy we're hunting in their territory."

5

Whycocomagh

The shorter days and chilly autumn air, together with the wandering clouds of fog over the water, heralded the coming winter. The *Rameurs* had much to do to prepare for that harsh season and not much time to do it.

Excited with his new map, Hector consulted it to check the distance to Whycocomagh. "We should reach the Mi'kmaq village in two days. I'm thankful we're on our way at last." He glanced with displeasure at the two dawdling rabbit hunters.

Accustomed to water-bound travel, several *Rameurs* lost no time in approaching Frank. They wanted to see the Charles Perrault book. Aside from Bibles in church, books were rare items in Acadia. As Frank passed it around, there were many cries of wonderment at the illustrations. The book inspection done, he began to read "Little Red Riding Hood." Pleasure beamed from every face.

It was no surprise that protests were voiced when he moved on to other tasks. All pleaded for another tale. Pretending reluctance, Frank then obliged and read "Puss in Boots."

Nola was perhaps the most attentive while Frank recited. She could see the words on the pages as he read, but these were still mostly meaningless strings of letters to her. Nola felt her illiteracy sharply. It cut her off from a world of beautiful ideas. She vowed to devote every free moment to understand the logic behind those strings of letters.

"Frank, I'd like to borrow that book when you aren't using it," she said. "The sooner I learn to read, the fewer people will pester you. I could read for you."

"Don't think learning to read can be done on your own, Nola. It's not a simple task, or more people would be able to do it. For one thing, you need someone to show you the pronunciation key."

"Then give me pronunciation exercises and I'll practise."

"I'll be glad to do that. But you have to understand that learning to read takes time and perseverance."

"I've got both of those, Frank. Now please let me have that book."

At the beginning of October the flotilla made landfall in a deep bay about six miles from Whycocomagh. Here, Hector believed, they would find shelter, fresh water, and wood for fuel and building as well as easy access to the aboriginal village. He decided they would haul the four shallops over the narrow butte so they could row to the village. Their first contact with the Mi'kmaq would be critical, so Hector picked twelve persons he judged would make a good impression on their new neighbours. To reduce any suspicion the Mi'kmaq might have that they were a clandestine warrior group, he included four girls plus Grandpa, the only *Rameur* fluent in the Mi'kmaq language.

That afternoon their first glimpse of Whycocomagh caught them all by surprise. The village was huge, much larger than they had expected. From the water more than two hundred conical huts were visible. Each of these was about twelve feet high and was made of woven rush mats, sheets of bark, or animal skins. At the party's appearance fifty men, women, and children came down to the shore to watch. The tall, bronzed watchers remained silent and immobile, neither welcoming nor hostile. They weren't indifferent, but neither, curiously, did they appear to be much interested. The *Rameurs* were very nervous at this unexpected silence and made no move to go ashore.

Instinctively, Grandpa understood the situation, but it took him agonizing minutes to decide how to break the growing tension. Finally, he stood with bowed head and held tobacco leaves at arm's length. Using the Mi'kmaq language, he said in a voice as bold and strong as he could muster, "We're travellers from afar who seek shelter in your lands for the coming winter."

Slow smiles greeted these words, and in no time several Natives broke ranks and stepped down the rocky slope to help pull the shallops ashore. Almost all — men, women, and children — took a tobacco leaf offered by Grandpa, pulled out a clay pipe from hidden folds in their clothing, and were soon engulfed in smoke. When Grandpa told the Mi'kmaq the tobacco was a present from Monsieur and Madame Denys, they broke out in broader smiles and gestured amicably, indicating the great respect they had for the elderly couple.

Jocelyne and Nola approached a tall, well-built youth. Using the same stance Grandpa had, they offered the boy a jar of honey. The youngster accepted the gift and tasted its contents gingerly. The boy then identified himself as Toomy, son of Chief Toomy. He invited the girls to meet other members of his clan, starting with his father and mother.

Nola could see there was only a minor difference in the appearance of the chief's family teepee from those of other families. It was graced with a large, colourful drawing of an eagle. The chief was taller, had a more dignified bearing, and was more sturdily built than the other men, an indication, Nola thought, that he was probably a particularly successful hunter. Then Nola spotted several women stoking a campfire and placing several pieces of meat on the coals. "Perhaps," she said to Hector, "they're preparing a feast to welcome us."

And so it proved to be. Dinner preparations continued until the chief signalled for everyone to gather around. Sitting cross-legged, he sang what sounded like a benediction. When that was done, he made a sign that everyone should eat. Several, Nola observed, hadn't waited for the chief's signal. Apart from the meat, which tasted like moose steak, there was little else — only a few turnips, juniper berries, and cranberries. Later Nola discovered why that was so. The tribe maintained only a small vegetable patch, smaller she was surprised to note, than Madame Denys's garden.

"Despite having so few ingredients, that meal was tasty," Jocelyne said to Nola. "I think the cooks used a few herbs we should learn about."

After the meal, Toomy brought the girls over to the largest structure in the village, an attractive teepee of which he was clearly proud. Beautifully decorated with drawings and blankets, it appeared to serve double duty as both a house of prayer and a community centre.

But this relaxed and casual mood changed abruptly when Grandpa told Chief Toomy that their group was part of a larger band. The chief tensed and insisted on seeing the rest of the *Rameurs* immediately. A dozen canoes were launched to accompany Hector and his party back to their main camp.

Once at the *Rameur* landing site and noting the large number of interlopers, the chief's expression turned grave. In a stern voice he announced, "Our hunting grounds can't support the addition of so many mouths. We can't allow you to hunt our deer, moose, and bears. We would starve if we permitted that. We also can't allow you to trap our valuable fur animals like beavers, foxes, and minks. We use those for clothing and in trade with the white man for knives and other metal items."

"I was afraid of that," Grandpa said to Hector. "We're in trouble. He might kick us out."

Then the chief unexpectedly changed his tone. "But we're a generous people. You can trap small animals like rabbits and porcupines and shoot partridges, and you can catch all the fish you need. Respect our rules, and you can stay on our land this winter. You can also cut all the timber you need, and we'll help you hunt those animals that aren't part of our own needs."

The harsh reality of surviving in the bush was evident in the Mi'kmaq population: there were few elders. It seemed there was no one over forty years old. Survival, apparently, meant being able to provide for your own needs.

Having won the chief's reluctant approval, the little clan of refugees began the task of building winter quarters. Grandpa and Frank scoped out suitable construction materials, while Hector prepared foundations for ten huts. When Frank discovered that the banks of the nearby stream were made of oozy, muddy clay, he thought that might be used as caulking between spruce branches.

"Yes," Grandpa told him, "a structure like that should make good walls."

The floors wouldn't be a problem — just a flat dirt base covered with spruce boughs would be quite adequate. But building a suitable roof would prove to be far more complicated.

Grandpa's expertise in this area came in handy. "First," he said, "we need to cut four trees and place them as posts on the corners of each hut." He continued at some length to describe how to assemble pieces made of spruce boughs, branches, and mud as roof material. It was obvious that building things was one of Grandpa's great passions. "When those are dry, we'll raise them into position on the triangle frame by a crane mechanism we'll have to construct. A roof like that will be leak-proof as long as no one steps on it."

Hector nodded. "Sounds good."

"I like that, too, but how will we heat our huts?" Nola asked. "The Mi'kmaq build campfires in the middle of their teepees and let the smoke drift out at the top. But that makes the inside smoky."

"Yes, our Native friends do have a smoky smell about them," Jocelyne said. "I guess we, too, can smell pretty strong sometimes. Not so smoky, though."

"Actually," Grandpa said, "the Mi'kmaq have a good reason to like the smoke. It helps keep the mosquitoes away. Also, if they want to, they know how to build a double-walled teepee that drives the smoke upward."

"Maybe so," Frank said, "but if we build a chimney, that would provide more heat per fire log plus reduce the smoke. It would also mean fewer logs to cut. And we have the clay right here from our stream."

At the end of much discussion there was unanimous agreement: the less smoky, fewer fire logs design was the way they would go.

Everyone was so focused on building that when the huts were finished they were all taken aback, particularly after the many problems they had had assembling their rafts. Little Adele neatly summed up everyone's mood. "It's going to be so nice to sleep indoors. The nights are getting much too cold for sleeping outside."

A few days after this crucial goal was achieved, Toomy and his dog came by to visit. Nola asked Toomy the dog's name. She couldn't pronounce the vowels Toomy voiced. To her it sounded something like "Zena." So she called out, "Zena, over here, I have a snack for you." To her delight the dog approached, tail wagging, and took the piece of fish Nola offered. After eating it, the dog offered a paw for her to shake. Nola grinned. "I think I just made a new friend."

Toomy signed to Nola and Jocelyne to join him and Zena in his canoe. They climbed aboard, and he paddled about fifty feet offshore. He took out a spear stored in the bottom of his canoe and stood. Carefully, he scanned the cold water and within minutes managed to spear a lobster. He handed this prize to Nola, using the same gesture she had employed when she gave him the jar of honey. Nola smiled. "Thank you."

Toomy gestured that Nola should give spearing a try. She could only glimpse vague shapes through the murky water. "I can't see well enough for this, Jocelyne. You try." She handed her friend the spear.

It took Jocelyne twice as long as Toomy, but she succeeded at last. "It's tough, but I can do it." She placed her catch under her seat.

The three paddled over to Whycocomagh Bay where Toomy pointed at two long rows of sticks planted in the water perpendicular to the shore. The width between the sticks gradually narrowed. When the girls canoed over to the apex of this array, they saw that many fish had been caught behind a barrier net that stretched to the shore. Looking closer, Nola cried, "Ooh! There are only eels in that net. I don't like eels."

"I've tasted them," Jocelyne said. "They're oily and none too pleasant to eat."

Toomy could see his companions weren't pleased but made no gesture of acknowledgement.

After this excursion, they paddled back to their campsite and were enjoying the scenery when suddenly they realized that Zena was taking advantage of their inattentiveness. She was quietly munching away on their prized lobsters! Toomy called out roughly to his dog, but it was too late. Zena had eaten everything edible.

"Dogs will be dogs," Jocelyne said. "It's our fault for not watching her."

Nola nodded. "I think there's quite a bit of wolf left in that dog."

Toomy dropped them off with the suggestion that they come to his village for a visit.

For the next month the girls were too busy to follow up on Toomy's tempting invitation. Mostly, they tried different non-spear ways to catch lobster. But in the last week of October two events made a visit to the Mi'kmaq urgent: a driving snowstorm hit the encampment, a reminder that their water passageway to Whycocomagh would soon close, and they received an invitation to a special ceremony scheduled for the next afternoon. The refugees were so eager that at the crack of dawn the next day four shallops crammed with *Rameurs*, including Jocelyne, Nola, and Grandpa, went off to the Native community.

On the way Nola said, "We're making progress with those lobster traps. This morning when I checked the traps there were four in one alone. That's our best haul yet. I think that last design change Hector made did the trick."

"Most of the credit belongs to you, Nola," Frank said. "You made sure we persisted until we got a design that worked."

On arrival the guests were ushered into the House of Prayer teepee. The village elders, dressed in colourful attire, were dancing in a circle to the slow beat of drums and chanting a solemn refrain — a beautiful ritual. The autumn goose hunt had been successful. This celebration was the Native way of giving thanks.

Grandpa, the only *Rameur* to understand the lyrics, said, "The Mi'kmaq are a profoundly spiritual people. Even if you don't understand what's being sung, it's easy to see they're truly thankful for the bounty their gods have given them. They have a strong connection to the spirit world."

The thanksgiving dance was followed by storytelling. Grandpa interpreted what was being said. One tale told of a brave hunter named Glooscap with superhuman powers but who was often unlucky in the hunt because of an evil wizard's mischief. There was also an artful sorceress who alternated between helping Glooscap and frustrating him. In another story Glooscap had a big battle with the Ice King, who had brought a harsh winter that made Glooscap's people cold, hungry, and sick. Glooscap might have had great and powerful gifts, but he had limitations that made him a sympathetic, much-beloved hero.

The storytelling was followed by plates of a stew for everyone. After the meal, Jocelyne went to see the cook. With Grandpa acting as interpreter, she asked, "What makes your stew so tasty?"

In response the cook brought out an herb that Jocelyne immediately recognized as wild garlic. "So that's it. It adds a wonderful flavour to your stew. Thank you for telling me." She bowed in appreciation.

Grandpa translated the cook's response. "You must learn to let the land take care of you."

"That's a wise woman," Nola said. "Talking of wisdom, did you notice that even old Mi'kmaq people have healthy teeth? I think Native foods have a special quality that's missing in our food. In Acadia older people either lose most of their teeth or have a lot of cavities. I wonder why that happens."

"I don't know," Grandpa said, "but I've lost just about all my teeth, and those that I still have hurt like the devil. If the Natives have a 'secret ingredient,' I'd sure like to know what it is."

Toomy signalled the *Rameurs* to gather around. He proceeded to demonstrate how to make a snowshoe from deerskin and a single piece of pliable wood. The shoe he made was round like an animal's paw print and had sinews made from animal tendons, which were used to tie the skin to the wood.

Then Toomy cut a supple hardwood branch and shaped it into a six-foot-long bow so stiff that not one of the girls could flex it. This device was more familiar to the boys. The British had long forbidden Acadians to own muskets, so to compensate many had learned to make bows and arrows. It was the only weapon they had for hunting.

Showing he understood, Hector said, "I know that the best bows are taken from a hardwood that can be shaped so that the stretchy sapwood is on the forward side. It pulls back to its original shape and has the heartwood on the inside to help push it back."

Toomy had other members of his tribe help the refugees attempt these survival crafts, but most found them frustrating. Such tasks took great skill to do well. Only a few — Hector was one — had the dexterity to master this work. For most it would take the whole winter before they managed even a little competence. Frank was impressed by the technologies developed by the Mi'kmaq.

At dusk the *Rameurs* paddled back to their encampment contented. It had been an intense, lively day. As soon as they reached home, they collapsed onto their comfortable spruce bough beds and slept soundly.

Food at their encampment, dominated by cod and now lobster, was decidedly less appealing than the meat-rich fare available to the Natives. By the end of November, several *Rameurs* began to look quite gaunt — freezing temperatures were making food gathering from the sea more dangerous and difficult. Hector, the first to master the use of a bow and arrow while on snowshoes, went out hunting each day and usually managed to bring back a porcupine or two. Sometimes this was supplemented by a partridge, but he was always careful to obey the Chief Toomy's no-big-game rule, though more than once he was solely tempted to shoot a deer.

Each morning they now spied animal tracks in the snow. The most common belonged to rabbits and mice. Every few days Toomy dropped by with Zena. He demonstrated how to make and set snares to catch rabbits, and soon rabbit stew became a much sought after menu item.

Within a month their snare lines extended almost twenty miles into the bush. Even so, their traps produced fewer rabbits each day, far less than the demand. Everyone knew this catch would only get worse as the winter progressed. It was becoming clearer why only the strong survived the harsh winter.

When a storm lasting a week shut down all food gathering, Jocelyne complained bitterly. "Everybody's half starved. These storms are so powerful they seem like vengeance from God. Have we done something wrong? If this continues, by Christmas we'll be starving."

Nola considered their situation thoughtfully. She wondered if they could trap the rabbits alive. If they could, perhaps they could start a colony just as they had kept chickens back at Grand Pré. She decided to approach Hector with this idea.

Hector frowned. "If you can find some rabbit bait, I can try to rig a trip box that might catch them, but it won't be easy."

"We don't have any carrots left, and that's their favourite food. But I saw some rabbits munching on seaweed the other day. Perhaps that would work as bait."

For the next few days Nola and Hector tried different trap designs and baits, but had no success. "I knew this wouldn't be easy," he groused.

One day, shortly after this disappointment, Toomy came by with his dog. He chuckled when he saw what they were attempting. Although he had never done any live trapping himself, he was excited by the challenge and had an excellent suggestion. Perhaps Zena could be trained to chase the rabbits into the live traps.

"That dog's too smart for that," Hector said. "It's her instinct to kill her prey."

"Yes," Nola said, "but Toomy has a good idea. If we're patient and practise every day, Zena could be trained to obey a new command. Training dogs to do new tricks is all about routines. As you said, she's smart. I wager you my share of our next rabbit stew that I can do it."

"It's a bet."

Now that Nola's pride was at stake, she sat next to Zena and had a little chat. "I need your help, Zena. We know you're good at chasing rabbits, but now you have to learn a new trick. You have to catch them without killing them." Zena licked Nola's hand, sat on her haunches, and offered a paw. Nola shook the dog's paw. "I knew you'd understand, Zena. We have a deal. Now let's practise." As they went off to the trap lines, Zena wagged her tail with great enthusiasm.

Hector was right. It *was* tough. But after only two weeks, Toomy was also correct. Bit by bit, Zena got more proficient, and finally, one afternoon just before Christmas, she succeeded. She chased a rabbit straight into a live trap. Nola beamed with delight. "Good, Zena! Good girl!"

After that first success, others came quickly. By the first week of the new year, they had twenty rabbits corralled in a pen built of ice walls on three sides. The side of Nola's hut served as the fourth wall.

Hector was gracious in defeat. "Here, Nola, you can have my rabbit stew. We might not have much output from your rabbit scheme for a while, but it's certainly put everyone in a more hopeful frame of mind."

"Thank you, Hector, but the credit really belongs to Zena, so I'm giving her your stew."

Zena ate Hector's portion with such relish that even he had to respond with a wistful grin.

Managing a rabbit hutch proved to be a lot of work. Each day Nola and twenty girls had to gather food for the hutch and clean the pens. Since deep snow covered most of the regular rabbit fare, she devised a method, using their rafts, to harvest sea moss and kelp, but this was cold, dangerous work. Then the moss and kelp had to be washed in fresh water before the rabbits would eat it. But these labours met with notable success. Slowly, steadily, their rabbit colony grew, and all agreed it was worth the effort. Every time the *Rameurs* ate farmed rabbit stew, Nola felt a flash of pride. Now when storms hit they were still hungry but were instilled with hope that things would soon get better.

Flushed with this accomplishment, Nola decided she would record the event by drawing a picture of a rabbit. Toomy helped by preparing a large piece of birchbark for the picture panel, while Nola made a variety of the charcoal sticks she would need — big, small, hard, and soft ones. The resulting drawing pleased everyone. It depicted an attractive, long-eared rabbit sitting on its haunches in deep snow. Nola was so proud of the picture that she signed it with her formal name — Noella — together with the year, 1756. Her rabbit feat and enthusiasm had given the *Rameurs* encouragement just when it was most needed.

Frank's lessons continued to be popular, though the shortage of writing surfaces was a problem. One day in mid-January, acutely frustrated at this lack, he made a strange suggestion. "Monsieur Denys's map shows that just twenty miles from here, where the lake narrows, there's a gypsum deposit. Gypsum's a fairly soft stone, so we might be able to shape it to make a flat surface for writing."

Hector nodded. "Many of us are definitely irritated at this writing surface problem. We have the time and some of us have become good at using snowshoes, so even a fairly long trip could be managed."

"And, of course, let's not forget such a trip would be an adventure," Frank added.

Three days later a party of twenty boys set off to the little narrows. Several girls pleaded to join the group, but Hector, to their great annoyance, said no. There was too much work to be done at camp.

"Hector isn't being fair to us girls," Jocelyne grumbled.

While the gypsum crew was away, Nola and Jocelyne introduced an Order of Good Cheer modelled on Samuel de Champlain's first winter in Acadia. Each evening one of four groups put on various entertainments such as dances, plays, or storytelling. It was a great way to have fun and to soothe hurt feelings at being denied going on the trip, not to mention a good way to divert attention from concern about the welfare of the gypsum crew.

After two weeks, with no word from the gypsum crew, the Good Cheer activities started losing their appeal. Most *Rameurs* felt it was time to ask Toomy to launch a search party. Toomy's mission was just getting underway when at long last the gypsum crew returned.

"They're back!" Adele shouted. "We were getting real worried. What kept you so long?"

Pointing at a toboggan, Frank said, "Working that gypsum proved to be far tougher than we expected. The first snag was that we had to heat the stone to make it flat."

"Notice that our boards are black," Hector said. "The first ones we made were so white you couldn't even see the chalk lines. Joseph and Remy found a soft black stone, and using a mortar and pestle, I turned that stone into a fine black powder that we worked into the gypsum."

"What took the most time," Frank added, "was that even after we made the gypsum flat and black, it was too soft to write on. We had to add lime as a stiffener, and that meant we had to burn limestone — not an easy thing to do in the winter. But none of us would give up, and we finally got the job done. Here, try one out."

Nola took a slate and a chalk stick and drew a picture of a fearsome rabbit chasing a terrified Zena. This improbable scene drew roars of laughter. In no time, other artists were drawing fanciful scenes, including one of a bear being pursued up a tree by a moose, of Grandpa riding on the back of a walrus, and one of Glooscap wrestling with the Ice King.

"I didn't know we *Rameurs* were so imaginative," Jocelyne said. "It's sure nice to have those slates."

"Yes, those slates bring out the storytellers in us," Nola said. "When I learn to write better, that's what I want to do — write stories and draw pictures to illustrate those tales."

— \ —

By mid-March, the first signs of spring — fresh shoots of greenery — began to appear wherever the snow had melted. Jocelyne and Nola went about the campsite selecting the most edible-looking of these buds and soon had a fragrant "weed soup" cooking. Their broth proved so tasty that everyone hankered for a second bowl.

"If we throw a couple of lobsters into that soup, I bet Frank will compare us to the best chefs in Europe again," Jocelyne said.

A week later the spring weather was sufficiently advanced that Hector announced to Chief Toomy that the *Rameurs* would be on their way within the week. "Your people have been very kind to us. We'll be forever in your debt. As we promised last fall, it's time for us to seek a place far from your hunting grounds."

Chief Toomy acknowledged this thanks and, gesturing, asked what the *Rameurs* were going to do with the many rabbits they had raised. Would they be taking them all on the rafts?

"No," Hector said, "there are too many. It would be our pleasure to give you a dozen or so."

When Grandpa discussed the transfer of the rabbits with Chief Toomy, he was surprised to discover that the Mi'kmaq wouldn't continue the rabbit farming. Apparently, it wasn't the traditional way. Also, though they were interested and somewhat impressed by the advantages of chimneys, Grandpa was told they wouldn't build those, either.

Frank tried to grasp their reasoning. "The Mi'kmaq are so accustomed to their traditional ways that even when something better comes along they're reluctant to accept it. It's really hard to understand why that's so. Perhaps sometime in the far past change meant something bad about to happen and it became taboo to accept it. Grandpa says that in the Mi'kmaq language the word for change carries a negative undertone."

"Maybe," Nola said, "but I believe if they had more iron tools they'd also be more open to change. Hard times have made them careful about adopting unproven methods. And, remember, even their smoky, no-chimney teepees help them fend off mosquitoes. Who are we to say what's best?"

The next day Toomy came by. In his arms he held a lovely surprise for Nola. "This is for you," he gestured. It was a lively pup the spitting image of Zena.

Taking the pup in her arms, Nola cried, "You're so beautiful! You have the same brown, black, and white as your mother and have the same expressive ears. Thank you, Toomy. Thank you very much." She went over and have him a big hug. "What a wonderful present. Let's see. I wonder what we should call him." Thinking for a moment, she answered her own question. "I know. I'm going to name him Zoopie. The *Z* sound will remind us of his delightful mother."

Nola could tell Toomy was genuinely pleased. He promised her he would come visit Zoopie, and all the *Rameurs*, when they found a new place to live.

The shallops and rafts were readied for the new voyage, food and water was loaded onboard, and Jocelyne brought her precious beehive. Remy, Joseph, and Pierre tightened the rope holding the bayonets to their spears and checked their other fishing gear. Wood for cooking was stacked in the centre of the rafts, enough flints for lighting fires were found, and all their clothes and blankets were packed. Then Hector announced, "We're ready!"

Once on the water, the *Rameurs* waved heartily to the hundred or so Mi'kmaq gathered to see them off.

6

Westmount and Louisbourg

The flotilla made its first stop, quite unanticipated, only three hours into the trip. It was to check gypsum outcroppings that Frank had sighted along the shore. Several of the refugees with no writing slates had insisted on taking advantage of this opportunity to make their own slate. Slate shortages were the source of much bad feeling, particularly when the treasured drawings of one "artist" had to be erased by another.

Frank was more than willing. "I noticed that gypsum bubbles up when it's heated. I'd like to find out what those bubbles are made of."

"How are you going to check that?" Jocelyne asked.

"I'm going to taste it."

Quite astonished, Nola said, "I hope it's not poison-ous." Frank had a directness and sharpness of mind that intrigued her. It seemed that he was forever trying strange —to her — ways to understand how things worked.

Hector also had a reason to stop. "I'm going to try to find a quicker way to grind that black shale. Last time we used a mortar and pestle, and it was slow work. I think if I attached a shaft and pedal mechanism to a piece of granite the grinding would become much easier."

Unlike their earlier efforts, this conversion of gyp-sum into slates went swiftly. It took just over two days, and everyone pitched in with renewed energy when they found an ample supply of seashells. "These seashells are certainly easier to convert into lime than the hard lime-stone we used before," Frank said.

By noon of the third day, everyone was delighted to possess, finally, their very own slate. Then it was time to get back onto the rafts.

As they were about to leave, Frank loaded so many gypsum rocks onboard that Hector became concerned they might sink. "Why on earth do you want so many of those rocks, Frank?"

"I have a project in mind," Frank said mysteriously. "But don't ask me what it is yet, because I'm not sure it will work."

Grandpa changed the subject. "I think we should head for the eastern arm of the lake. It's about twenty miles from here and looks as if it would only be a four-mile portage to reach the tip of that arm to the head of the Baie des Espanols. That's the bay where Monsieur Denys's map shows there's an outcrop of coal."

Hector nodded but then asked, "Frank, how do you plan to move all that rock over the portage?"

"Well, I was planning to talk to you about that. I hope there will be a good trail along that portage, good enough to support a wheel. If that's what we find, I'd like you to ask some boys to build a few wheelbarrows."

"If the trail's smooth enough, then fine, yes. But why don't you tell us more about how you plan to use all that stone?"

"I told you. I'm not sure my plan will work. There are several things that could go wrong, so I'd rather not talk about it until I know more."

It was well past midnight and so dark when they landed at the head of the eastern arm that no one dared venture ashore for fear of getting lost. First light showed a dense forest of spruce and pine covered with smoke-like haze floating among the treetops. It soon became apparent that there was a well-used trail along one side of a rocky gully.

"Monsieur Denys's map shows no settlement around here, so I expect that trail was made by Mi'kmaq hunters," Hector said. "We'll leave the rafts here and portage our supplies and the shallops. It's only ten miles to that coal outcropping. It shouldn't be too difficult to ferry all our supplies in those boats."

Frank was so anxious to see the outcropping that he rushed ahead, carrying only a light load. This resulted in him being the first to see the small inlet that would become the new home of the *Rameurs*. By the time others had joined him, he had made a preliminary assessment.

"I think we should build along this flat area next to the creek," Frank told them. "It's close to that coal seam." He pointed. "And there are lots of seashells and clay for building. Plus those red rocks Monsieur Denys mentioned are in the hill just half a mile away. But we'll have to start a forest fire to create an open space around our settlement. We don't want anyone to sneak up on us."

"Why the fire?" Nola asked. "Do you think someone might attack us?"

"It's just a precaution, Nola. We don't need big protective walls but, as you well know, we live in a dangerous world and must prepare proper defences."

Hector was annoyed that Frank was taking the lead, but he couldn't argue with the English boy's reasoning, so he gave the order to protect their supplies, then the go-ahead for the burn.

Embers were still crackling when they set to work cutting trees for their new cabins. These structures were meant to be permanent, so they would be built on a more comfortable scale than their cramped huts at Whycocomagh. Still, there would be some twelve *Rameurs* per cabin.

As this work started, Grandpa suggested a name for their new outpost. "Let's call it Rougemount after the red rock in the surrounding hills."

"There isn't that much red rock," Hector said. "In fact, it's mostly dull grey."

Frank piped in. "I do like the idea of 'mount' in the name. The hill is obviously there, and we're on the western side of the bay. So I think a good name would be Westmount."

Other ideas for names bounced back and forth with so much enthusiasm that Hector decided the only fair way to resolve the matter was to vote. It was close, but by the end of their second day at the site, with nothing yet erected, their new settlement had a name. They called it Westmount.

Jocelyne and Grandpa searched for a good spot to place their beehive, which was difficult since no meadows existed around Westmount. That was a deficiency that would also limit the community's prospects for a garden.

Grandpa pointed at the flat land across the bay. "There should be lots of bee food on that side. In fact, I can see some flowers from here."

"That does look like a good place," Jocelyne said. "Let's take a shallop over to check it out."

As they rowed over with the hive, Grandpa counselled Jocelyne. "Remember that the beehive is a highly organized little world. All bees work for the benefit of the whole colony, not the individual. We must keep in mind that keeping bees in hives is for the benefit of the beekeeper, not the bees. When I kept bees, I always tried to be in tune with their needs, not mine."

Back at the settlement, Nola busied herself building proper pens for the rabbits. Rabbits were avid diggers, so it was essential to build the pens on a hard base. Zoopie accompanied Nola everywhere she went. The pup was still too young to learn rabbit-herding skills, but other tricks, under Nola's patient instruction, came easily. Zoopie proved to be good at stick retrieval, rolling over, and paw shaking. Nola understood instinctively that dogs depended on the kindness of others for their very existence, so she knew how to get the best out of her dog. "He's quite smart but can't talk, so any scolding for naughty behaviour has to be balanced by lots of praise for accomplishments," she told Frank.

After three days of frenzied building activity, Hector called for a celebration rest. They only had a few cod, lobster, and shellfish but, cooked with succulent herbs Jocelyne had found in the beehive meadow, this sparse fare proved to be a hit. She also tried her hand at making boiled seaweed "salad," but that was a disaster.

"Better let the rabbits eat that stuff," Hector suggested ruefully.

After the meal, a few *Rameurs* were still energetic enough to play flutes and tambourines to entertain the weary crew. This merriment was in full swing when Grandpa, relaxing on a stump away from the main group, noticed a couple of shallops emerge on the far side of the bay. These soon proved to belong to Acadian settlers who were displeased at the arrival of the *Rameurs*.

Without even a civil greeting, a man in the lead shallop shouted, "This is our land! You can't stay here. No campsites are allowed. Interlopers aren't welcome. You have to leave right now."

Dismayed and surprised at this belligerent attitude, Hector replied in an equally harsh tone. "There wasn't a soul here when we arrived, and there was no evidence anyone had ever lived here. You obviously have your own land somewhere else. Why are you being so selfish? There's room for all."

"This whole area was given to us by the governor at Louisbourg. We won't stand for trespassers on our land. You must get off!"

Hector glared at them. "Well, we'll have to talk to the governor about that, won't we? Now you push off yourself! We don't like your kind around here!"

This nasty dispute put a damper on the celebrations, and before long all attempts at restarting the music died out. Several refugees went back to work, though not in a happy frame of mind.

"I don't remember any family being so greedy in Grand Pré," Nola said.

Frank attempted to persuade Hector to assign several boys to work with him on his mysterious project. "I'd like to build a special heating box for the coal."

"You can do your tinkering when the essentials are done, Frank," Hector said, still unhappy about the English lad's seeming attempts to lead their band. "We need to concentrate on getting coal to heat our cabins."

"We can do both, Hector. My project wouldn't slow us down from getting coal for our regular needs, not by much, anyway."

Hector ignored him. Instead, he assigned a work crew to dig into the coal outcropping. Within a few hours they produced a shoulder-high heap of coal. He then instructed his team to build clay fireplaces in each cabin.

The next week the occupants of every cabin took pleasure in a wonderful new phenomenon — a lovely coal fire. "Coal sure beats wood as a way to heat our cabins," Hector said. "A little goes a long way."

Frank wouldn't give up his heating box project. In his spare time he built a strange-looking structure. It had a double-barrelled chimney — a heating box placed inside a regular chimney — with the heating box connected to a pipe that arced back to ground level.

"It's a way to heat coal without burning it," he explained to Nola. "The pipe allows you to condense any vapour that evaporates from the hot coal. I've seen equipment like this in the wine-growing areas of France when they distill wine to make cognac. They call them distillation towers. All I'm doing differently is to heat coal instead of wine."

"That's an odd project," Nola said, "but I'd be happy to help once I get the rabbit hutches and lobster traps going. I think it's nice you're using ideas from France."

"Lots of people in many countries have known about distillation for two or three hundred years."

Frank accepted Nola's help happily, but she was the only one, so it took more than two weeks to make a proper distillation tower, a delay he found profoundly frustrating. Then, when this work was mostly done, he realized he had to wait some more for the mud to dry. "We can test the tower only when the mud dries, or the heat will cause it to crack. I think we'll be ready by this time tomorrow. Then I'll need to scrounge a bit of the coal from Hector to test it."

The next day an anxious Frank touched his tower every hour. By late afternoon, he judged it dry enough to start the first run. He had managed to secure some wet coal from Hector, but this material proved difficult to light. After much patience, he finally got it to burn satisfactorily. It produced a bluish flame that created far more heat than he had anticipated. "That's a lovely fire indeed," he said to himself. "Maybe it's the wet that gives it that nice blue colour. Now let's see if there's anything in our condenser."

A strong, resinous aroma, unfamiliar and none too pleasant, surrounded the tower — a signal that the intense heat was indeed producing something. Holding his nose close to the condenser, Frank tingled. "That smells just like pine tar and turpentine." He paused for a moment, then took a sample of the newly condensed liquid and threw it into the coal fire. It immediately burst into a brilliant red flame.

"That's amazing!" several passing boys cried when they witnessed this event.

Frank was overjoyed. "Marvellous. That's exactly what I hoped would happen. My condenser works! It's just as my father told me. Fortune favours the bold."

That evening the *Rameurs* experienced something even more exciting than a coal fire — illumination by coal oil. To Nola this lamplight was a strangely satisfying type of elemental force. It made her so happy that she stayed up to read the Perrault book far into the night. This action resulted in a heated commotion in her cabin.

"Turn out that light, Nola," her irate cabin mates whispered. "It's halfway to morning. Go to bed."

By the end of June, little Westmount looked like a real settlement. There were now fifteen cabins, some with tiny "windows" made of scraped rabbit skin, and work had begun on a larger structure that would serve as their community centre.

After the unpleasant encounter with the Acadian settlers, Grandpa and Jocelyne decided to go back to the other side of the bay to hide their beehive. "Those greedy louts might destroy it," Grandpa said before they left.

When they arrived on the other side, Jocelyne said, "I was hoping we could use the meadows on this side as a garden, but we can't risk that now. However, there are a few fertile patches by the side of our creek that we could seed."

"You'd better keep a few of those seeds in reserve in case that ground won't support crops," Grandpa cautioned. "It's a long way back to Monsieur Denys's place if we run out of seeds."

Not long after Grandpa and Jocelyne returned from their mission, a large fishing schooner was spotted. The ship anchored in the bay close to the settlers. The mariners rowed ashore with an open, friendly demeanour and were accorded, in consequence, a cheerful reception.

"Welcome to our little community," Hector said. "We're glad to see you. Yours is the first fishing boat we've seen."

The sailors were Basques who, it turned out, had fished these waters for many years. Very outgoing people, they offered the *Rameurs* fresh haddock and, most surprisingly, a few pineapples and coconuts they had purchased from southern traders. In return the *Rameurs*, under Jocelyne's supervision, cooked them the best meal in her repertoire.

The Basques were intrigued by the coal oil lamps and indicated these would be very valuable in Europe. "That lamp oil would be worth a fortune in Spain," the captain told them.

"If you're interested, you could have a few barrels of coal oil and in exchange next season you could bring us back some things we need."

The captain was very interested, and for the rest of the Basques' stay, talk all over Westmount was focused on what things the *Rameurs* could get in return for their coal oil.

"I have to admit that Frank's contraption produced something valuable," Hector said.

In mid-July, Jocelyne approached Hector and Frank with a problem caused by success. The beehives were producing so much honey that storing it had become challenging. "I don't have enough containers to hold it all," she said. "For now I'm just using the honeycombs, but that won't do for much longer."

Drawing from his experience at making gypsum slates, Frank said, "I have just the thing for that. You know those gypsum rocks we brought on the rafts? Well, we can heat them up, mix in some burnt seashells, and add a little water to form a thick mass that will harden into whatever shape you want — not just a flat surface. It would be fairly easy to make a container that could hold several gallons."

Not to be outdone, Hector added, "I have something to help also. I connected one of our bayonets to a foot-operated treadle that lets me turn wood into all sorts of round shapes. I could make goblets to hold drinks. It's a wonderful little machine. I can make any round shape."

"You boys are so inventive," Jocelyne said. "How can I help you make those things?"

"No," Hector said. "You go ahead and make something interesting with that honey. How about a honey wine? Frank and I will make you some containers."

A culinary challenge always excited Jocelyne. She tried different ingredients, and within a couple of weeks produced mead flavoured with dandelion flowers and leek roots.

"This is a lot better than spruce beer," she announced to Nola, "but I think it still needs a bit of work. You think garlic would help?" She was soon operating a modest canteen outside her cabin door, serving goblets of her rough drink. Together with a shellfish snack made from pickled winkles, this made her canteen a popular place.

At the end of July, Toomy came by with his dog. The reunion of Zena and her son gladdened the hearts of all who saw the event. After a bit of growling and sniffing, Zena suddenly realized Zoopie was her son and began to howl with joy. That was followed by much play-wrestling and running around — a great treat for both canine and human.

Hector was keen to settle their land dispute problem, so just before August, when it was apparent their garden wasn't going to produce enough seeds for next year's planting, they agreed it was high time to visit Louisbourg. Many *Rameurs* wanted to go on the excursion, but as with the initial encounter with the Mi'kmaq at Whycocomagh, Hector wanted a carefully controlled first meeting. He decided that only one shallop would make the trip, and that he, Jocelyne, Nola, Sammy — the younger brother of Leo, the boy slain during the fight when crossing the isthmus — and Zoopie would go.

The weather was perfect for sailing as the shallop set off on the nearly fifty-mile sea journey to the fortress. The boat handled well even when the ocean breeze made the vessel heel over. Hector figured they might reach the fortress before nightfall.

Zoopie was sitting by Sammy's side when they saw

the first dolphins of the voyage. Dolphins were curious animals that liked to swim along unusual things such as boats. Zoopie got excited at this interesting "big fish" and began a frenzied barking spree. Sammy had to calm him down. "These are friendly animals, Zoopie. There's no need to be afraid."

The dog seemed to understand. "Friends," he barked, then sat. Soon he was back to his specialty of napping.

The horizon was barely visible by the time the shallop turned past the harbour lighthouse and into Louisbourg Bay. The huge grey walls were lit by only a few lanterns, so they managed to pull up right to the dock unobserved by the night guard.

Hector whistled boldly to a guard. "Hey, sleepyhead, wake up. You've got visitors."

The guard, embarrassed at not noticing them earlier, asked gruffly, "Who are you?"

"We're from a new settlement in the Baie des Espanols area. We escaped from the British at Grand Pré and would like to meet the governor."

"Oh, you're welcome then. But you'll have to wait until the morning to meet the governor. You can sleep in the guardhouse tonight."

"Thank you. You haven't any food, do you? Our fishing line broke and we haven't eaten any dinner."

"I'll see what I can do. That's a cute little dog you have there."

In the morning the head of the guards treated the visitors kindly. He brought them to Pierre Lorant's L'Hôtel de la Marine for a hearty breakfast of meat pie, cabbage, sausage, and heavy brown bread. Then he escorted them up the cobblestoned street to the huge edifice called the King's Bastion and past the white-and-gold chapel right into the governor's office.

Governor Augustin de Drucour, descended from a long line of Norman knights, greeted them cordially. He was quite impressed when they presented him with a coal oil lamp and demonstrated its power of illumination.

"Very remarkable indeed," he told them. Then he asked Madame Drucour to join them so he could show her the *Rameur* innovation.

Madame Drucour asked Jocelyne and Nola about their adventures and how they were doing. When Jocelyne explained about their garden problems, Madame Drucour said, "I'll be glad to supply you with the seeds you need, but you'll have to ask the governor about your land problem. Here, I want to show you angelica, my favourite plant. It looks like umbrella ribbing, and we use it as medicine against colds, bronchitis, and rheumatism. We eat the roots and leaves as a vegetable and make jams and jellies from it. The roots are also good as a yellow dye."

"Oh, I hope we can get some of those seeds, too," Nola said.

The governor had some dreadful news. France and Britain were once again at war. Several battles had already taken place in New York, Ohio, India, and Germany. Hector gasped as the governor related the barbarity the battles had inflicted on both defenders and combatants. Then he regained his composure enough to ask the governor to deed them the land on which Westmount was built plus have gardening rights to the meadows across the bay.

"If you pay ten percent of your coal oil output to the crown, then you'll get the land," the governor said.

Hector didn't hesitate. "We accept those terms."

The next day Hector and his crew were escorted back to Westmount by two whaleboats full of soldiers. Governor Drucour wanted to be certain the unruly settlers threatening the *Rameurs* wouldn't do so again.

Frank was understandably concerned when he learned of the new war between France and his homeland. It was time to put a plan he had been considering into effect. "Hector, we need help to make a weapon to defend ourselves."

"What do you have in mind?"

"You know how we've been making containers from that gypsum mix? Well, it's also possible to make two containers, one fitting inside the other."

"What's the value in that?"

Frank grinned. "The inside piece can move up and down as a piston in a cylinder-shaped outside container. So if you place, say, coal oil in the cylinder, the piston can push the liquid down through a pipe at the bottom and squirt it out."

"Yes, I can see that. If the piston were attached to a lever, you could get a fair amount of pressure in the pipe."

Frank clapped Hector on the back. "That's right. And if you light the coal oil as it leaves the pipe, you get a stream of fire to spray at the enemy. It's called Greek fire. I learned about it at school."

"Sounds like a brutal weapon. I guess that was why you wanted all that gypsum rock, but why didn't you tell us about your plan?"

"I had to make the distillation of coal oil work first, and I wasn't sure that would succeed. Making new things is always an uncertain process. It involves a lot of trial and error."

On September 10 the *Rameurs* marked the first anniversary of their escape from Grand Pré with a solemn ceremony. There being no priest available, Grandpa led the residents of Westmount in prayer:

> "Let us now bow our heads and join hands to remember our kin who suffer in faraway lands.
>
> O God, thou art a strong tower of defence to all that flee unto thee. Please save our kin from the violence of the enemy.
>
> O Lord, help our loved ones out of misery.
>
> Glory be to the Father, and to the Son, and to the Holy Ghost.
>
> As it was in the beginning, is now, and ever shall be, world without end. Amen."

The refugees' problems with the governor began shortly after their Louisbourg visit. French soldiers were attracted, no doubt, by the young ladies of Westmount as well as by the mead at Jocelyne's canteen, so they began to visit the little settlement. It was, after all, only thirty miles by land from Louisbourg. That by itself posed no difficulty. They became alarmed only when several men refused to go back to the fortress.

When the *Rameurs* asked the soldiers why they wouldn't return, the answer was shocking. Apparently, soldiers in the lower ranks were often exploited by their officers. Some became so fed up that they were ready to desert their posts. A particularly outrageous example was the case of Private Jodocus. The private's commanding officer forced him to work on his farm, taking care of his animals, growing hay, and clearing away firewood, all for absolutely no compensation. This involuntary "assistance" didn't improve the private's morale or his military skills.

Frank was outraged when he heard this. "No wonder they want to desert. That's no way to treat subordinates. If I were in their position, I'd do the same thing. We have the same problem in England, but only by a few rogue officers. And when those men are caught, they're severely punished."

One late-winter afternoon Hector and Frank stared, with growing disbelief, as a battalion of soldiers advanced on Westmount. Hector pulled out his spyglass and announced, "I was afraid it would come to this. Drucour has launched an expedition to bring back those deserters. That battalion looks fearsome. This is a serious business, Frank."

"Yes, but we have a good defensive position. I think we can handle them. I'm pleased to report that our pumps are ready. Our biggest pump can squeeze a gusher of fire more than thirty feet. When they get within range, we can let them have a taste of it."

Drucour's soldiers advanced, grimly purposeful, with muskets cocked.

"People are going to get killed," Nola said with foreboding.

On Hector's signal the primed pumps spurted a torrent of flames — dazzling bright and brutally hot — directly in front of the attackers. This torrent disrupted their advance, but only for a moment. They rallied and responded with a ferocious volley of musket fire that battered the row of fence posts hiding the fire machines. Peeking over the posts, Hector shouted, "That's just a taste of what we've got! You see we can defend ourselves. Let's sort this out like civilized people. Let's talk."

After a short hesitation, Drucour raised a green parley flag.

Hector opened the negotiations with a brutal accusation. "The way you allow your officers to exploit your men is disgraceful. That's a stupid way to run an army."

"Watch who you're calling stupid, young man, or I'll call this parley off right now."

"You're right, Governor. I apologize. Let's review each man's grievance one by one to see if we can arrive at a just solution."

"I'm ready to discuss, with proper decorum, any instances where my officers might have overstepped their authority," Drucour said. "But understand this. The British are blockading our ships as we speak. I can't allow any dereliction of duty. Now let us start with the Private Jodocus case."

Case by case was painstakingly reviewed, and where accommodations could be made that was done. After many hours of negotiations, Hector had to accept that thirty-five of the fifty deserters would have to return to Louisbourg. Private Jodocus was one of the few who won the right to stay. And Hector had to agree to return any future deserters immediately.

With that arrangement an amicable, if tense, resolution to the crisis was achieved. Drucour prepared to leave. As the line of soldiers faded into the distance, Nola approached Frank. "I'm glad that's over. Soldiers, French or English, aren't my favourite people. By the way, how did you get those pumps to squirt the coal oil so far?"

"It's all a matter of leverage, Nola. A ten-foot-long pole attached to a piston multiplies the force placed on it by a factor of ten. This generates enough pressure and can send a terrifying gusher of fire at the enemy. This principle was established long ago by a wise old Greek called Archimedes."

"You're so lucky to have gone to school and learned all those things. I'm very angry with my own people for not having the foresight to build schools in Acadia. None of us even knew how to write until you came. That wasn't smart on our part. Let me tell you, if I ever have children, they're going to be properly educated!"

7
Amazing Excitement

The addition of fifteen adult males to the social mix at Westmount changed its dynamic. Although Hector kept the new men busy digging for coal, running the distillation tower and, on two occasions, sending them off to the little quarry on the Bras d'Ors to get more gypsum, it was apparent there was competition for female company.

Jocelyne, chief beekeeper, principal person responsible for the production of mead, and hostess of the canteen, bore the brunt of this challenge. She confided to Nola. "I don't know if it's just my mead, but those new men seem to hang around me a lot these days. Most of the time I rather like it. The attention is nice as long as they don't get drunk."

"You're a good-looking young woman," Nola said. "It's not surprising that young men pay attention to you."

Hector, thinking about the need to store more coal oil, decided to build a large potter's wheel that would make it easier to create barrel-sized containers. Placing a slurry of gypsum-lime on this wheel enabled him to make excellent thin-walled containers.

"It's a lot easier to make big containers that way than by hand," he told Frank, "and it's much better than using pottery mud. There's no need to build a large kiln to bake the mud."

By mid-June, when the Basque fishermen returned, Hector had made many of these barrels. The Basques had brought bolts of wool cloth, orange marmalade, wheat, cloves, pepper, and most exciting for many of the newly literate among the *Rameurs*, twenty books on a variety of topics.

Looking over the books, Frank said, "These are splendid. We're going to make good use of them, particularly those encyclopedia volumes."

The arrival of the Basques prompted Frank to remember their vulnerability to attack from the sea. "Hector, we should build embankments along the shore of Westmount. It would hide our fire pumps."

"Frank's right," Grandpa said. "We need to be better prepared. We *Rameurs* come from a people who know a thing or two about building embankments. I can help the men place logs, mud, and rocks so they'll make a solid barrier against both water and anyone who might attack us."

"We're lucky to have you, Grandpa," Hector said. "It's a big job, but you're the best person to help us do it right. Go ahead and start. I'm going to build a catapult using a design I saw in one of those encyclopedias."

As this work progressed, everyone was optimistic except Frank. He realized their fire pumps weren't powerful enough to stop a determined attack. "It's certain that Drucour would have defeated us had he pressed his attack," he told Hector. "We haven't tried to do anything with that red rock yet. I'd like to look into that."

"Well, I must admit you were right with that coal tinkering. And the fire pump you made is impressive. Go ahead, Frank. If the red rock can be used to make something useful, we'd better find out. Just don't take too many people to do your tests. There are lots of other chores to be done around here."

Frank was excited to begin. He thought carefully about the scope of his project, then chose ten boys to use picks and shovels to pry pieces of the red stone from the surrounding bedrock. He banged some of this freed stone with a hammer and found it was harder than limestone but not so hard that he couldn't pound it into fine powder. "It's a lot softer than quartz," he told his workers. That done he got the boys to round up some coal and heated the powder. "It worked with the gypsum and limestone."

To his astonishment this resulted in a glossy black powder. "Actually, I shouldn't be surprised that something turns black when it's heated." He found the black substance had a strong taste, was quite a bit heavier than most rocks, and proved handy as a dye. Other than that he could see little use for it. He decided more heat might produce something more useful. Frank believed that the heaviness of the black powder was evidence there might be a metal hiding in the stone, and he knew liberating metals from rock took a lot of heat. Nola and the boys helped him to build a brick box around the powder, to add charcoal, and to fan the fire by blowing on it with a small bellows made from deer leather. When the powder turned white-hot, they saw something materialize that was truly remarkable.

"Hey, Hector, come over here!" Frank cried. "Have a look at this. See that metal in the bottom of the pot? It's iron. I'm very happy to say our red rock is made of iron!"

"Iron, huh?" Hector said. "We certainly could use more of that metal around here. We need axes, saws, hammers, shafts for wheels, all sorts of things."

"Yes, iron's useful for that, but it isn't something that we can use to defend ourselves. I'm going to continue my experiments."

Excited with this first success, Frank wondered what other things he could do with the black powder. "I'll try adding sea salt and heat that mixture to see what will happen," he said to Nola.

It seemed a simple matter to evaporate a few batches of sea water, but getting everything set up took more time than Frank expected. It was almost a full week before he had a small pile of dry salt.

The first heating of this new combination was a disappointment — nothing happened. "I'd better start keeping notes, or I'm going to lose my way," he mumbled to himself.

Nola overheard this mumbling and jumped in. "I can do that."

Frank knew he would probably have to do some spell-checking of her work, but was thankful and accepted her offer. Also, he mused, she was pleasant company. He decided to cover the ingredients with sand so that air couldn't affect the reaction. And he tried again.

Slowly, this test batch got hotter and hotter, but still there was nothing promising. Frustrated, he decided to remove the sand cover, add charcoal, and try once more. No sooner had this batch reached an orange colour than he saw red smoke rise. Delighted, he got his crew to help him build a condenser. "We've got to capture that red smoke!"

When the condenser was ready and had done its work, Frank realized they had actually made two new substances: The red powder distilled from the smoke easily dissolved in water, so he called it "red salt." There was also a new white powder. It was obviously different from the original sea salt, because when he added water it crackled and fizzled. The white powder had a sharp smell and felt slippery to the touch.

After a few tests, Frank recognized the new white substance as caustic soda. "It's lye, all right," he said. "It burns your mouth if you taste it and turns wood chips dazzling white. It's the same stuff you get when you leach water through wood ashes. We made soap by mixing this kind of soda with seal fat on the rafts."

"Yes," Nola said, "I remember doing that. We made a pretty good soap."

For several days Frank experimented with this red salt and lye mixture. He tried burning them with coal oil. He tried heating a combination of red salt with caustic soda, but it all produced nothing. Nola kept careful notes of every procedure.

"I love trying different things to see what works and what doesn't," Frank said to anyone who dropped by. "But it can be tough when you end up with nothing new. Still, I'd rather be reaching dead ends than not be trying at all."

Using several coal oil lamps to brighten his workspace, Frank often worked alone long into the night. But after two weeks he still had nothing — the red salt–lye combination only produced more ordinary salt. Irritated but not discouraged, he realized they were going in the wrong direction and asked to see Nola's notes.

Looking over them herself, Nola suggested he retrace his steps to the point where they had produced the white powder. "I see you didn't do anything with it except add water."

"You're right," he agreed.

Together they made a new batch of this dry white material, placed it in a pot, and put the pot on the fire. They were surprised to see pale yellow grains form. Frank found these grains puckered his nose when he smelled them and wrinkled the skin on his finger when he touched them. Then he found the substance absorbed water from the air so easily that he decided to keep it in a closed jar.

Nola, with Zoopie tagging along as usual, was with Frank the next day when he decided how to test this odd new material. "Here, Nola, would you hold this jar of coal oil while I add some of these yellow grains?"

She readily obliged and returned the jar. Secretly, she was beginning to wonder if Frank was wasting his time carrying out all these strange trials, but she knew he had a remarkable intuition about these matters and admired his persistence in the face of many dead ends. She continued to help and didn't complain or grumble.

"This might be dangerous," Frank warned. "I'm going to throw a hot ember into this new concoction. In fact, I hope it is dangerous, so please, Nola, step back a bit."

The instant Frank threw the hot ember into the concoction it erupted into an explosion powerful enough to knock him completely off his feet. Zoopie barked with fear. Concerned, Nola rushed over to Frank. "Are you all right? That was a mighty big blast."

Frank, dazed and flat on the ground, grabbed Nola. "I'm not just all right! I'm extremely all right! That new concoction is exactly what I was trying for."

In his excitement he hugged and kissed her roughly. Realizing what he had done, he backed off, embarrassed. "Uh, I'm sorry. I wasn't thinking."

Nola smiled broadly. "No, Frank, that was quite all right. In fact, I rather enjoyed it. You may kiss me again if you want."

"I ... I can? You mean you aren't angry with me?"

Modestly, yet with a twinkle in her eyes, she said, "On the contrary, Frank, I'm very happy you kissed me."

Frank didn't need another invitation. He kissed her again. Hard.

Zoopie growled at these strange goings-on and pulled so hard on Frank's shirt that it ripped half open.

With big smiles and a bounce in their step, Frank and Nola went off toward the settlement hand in hand. It didn't take long for the whole of Westmount to learn about the new relationship. Friends were soon giving the new couple congratulatory hugs.

"People are saying we're a good fit," Nola told Frank. "Isn't it nice to be a couple, dear?"

Frank responded with a smile and another kiss. "You're my girl, Nola."

Zoopie growled.

Hector stifled a scowl when he heard the news of this new relationship. It made him unhappy that Nola had succumbed to Frank's advances. Then he realized Jocelyne wasn't around. "I guess she must be across the bay tending either her beehives or the garden," he told Nola. "I'm going to go over to tell her about the big blast and about you and Frank."

Hector checked both the beehive and the garden areas but didn't see Jocelyne. Worried, he went deeper into the woods by the little stream that fed the garden, and there he saw her bathing. "Hello, Jocelyne, having fun?"

"Hector, get out of here! I don't have any clothes on."

"Oh, that's interesting. That's very interesting. I'll wait until you come out."

"Hector, I'm naked. Be a gentleman and let me get dressed."

"Who said I was a gentleman? I rather like looking at you like this. It's fun."

"You're being mean, Hector. I'm getting cold in here. Go away!"

"I'll tell you what. I'll turn around so you can get out without me looking."

Cold, and frustrated with Hector's shenanigans, Jocelyne leaped out and ran to her clothes. She got dressed quickly and then said, "You're a naughty man, Hector, but you are rather cute."

Hector turned around and kissed her. "I've wanted to do that for a long while. I'm glad you think I'm cute." Then he told her about Nola and Frank.

Jocelyne giggled at this news. "No wonder you were being so bold with me."

They rowed back to Westmount where they saw Frank and Nola sitting on an embankment clasping hands. Hector and Jocelyne walked toward them, holding their hands up. "We have news, too," Jocelyne said.

"Well, well, well, isn't this a nice surprise," Nola said. "It looks like this is quite a day for new relationships."

Frank and Hector were congratulating each other when Grandpa came over and said, "I see we have an unusually fine gathering here. Congratulations to all of you. By the way, Toomy just came over. He's at the main cabin looking at those iron tools Hector made last week."

Everyone went over to say hello to their Mi'kmaq friend and to tell him their news. Toomy, reserved as usual, still managed to convey his pleasure at the new relationships. Yet once the best wishes were said he and Grandpa discreetly moved out of hearing range and were then seen to engage in earnest discussion.

When they returned, Toomy said nothing and Grandpa evaded their questions despite considerable prodding by Jocelyne. "What were you two concocting back there? You're up to something. I can tell."

Inexplicably to the amorous four, Toomy was soon off back to Whycocomagh. "But you only just got here," Nola protested. "Zoopie has hardly had any time to play with Zena."

After Toomy left, Frank went back with Nola to check his chemical reactions. "What we're doing," he explained, "is called the 'art of heating.' You don't know in advance what will happen, so you heat each ingredient until it reaches a different colour and try this in different combinations. That yellow grain is great fun. I'm sure it's what makes the coal oil explode. I can tell from its pungent smell that the powder is strong bleach."

"It certainly surprised me that something so small could make such a big bang," Nola said. "It blew you right off your feet. I'm sure a larger amount would be very dangerous. I find it amazing that there's so much power hidden in a few rocks and some salt."

"Perhaps amazing, but real, and that's very good for us. I want to try a bigger amount, but don't worry. I'm going to take more precautions this time. Especially since we're mates." He grinned at her affectionately. "I want you to understand what I think is happening. The main ingredient in gunpowder, saltpetre, would just burn normally on its own, but when you add charcoal and sulphur, it burns so fast that it blows up. Our explosive is similar. The coal oil blows up because the bleach gives it something that it needs to burn with explosive force."

"Oh, Frank, please be careful."

One morning Frank and Nola were in the middle of preparing more bleach when Grandpa and twenty *Rameurs* came by and hustled the couple off without telling them what was up.

"Where are you taking us?" Frank demanded. "I don't like not knowing what's going on."

"No need to fret," Grandpa said. "We're going to take good care of you and Nola. Now come right this way." He pointed down the bay toward the Bras d'Ors.

They walked and sailed in a shallop the ten miles to the head of the eastern arm where they had first landed almost a year and a half earlier. Once there Frank and Nola were astounded to see that all eight rafts had been pulled together to make a large platform that stretched right across the arm and that on the shore enough trees had been felled to make even more space. They had only just arrived when they saw that Jocelyne and Hector were also being hustled along to the opening.

"Well, hello, fellow captives," Nola said.

"They won't tell us what's going on," Hector declared. "I protest."

The surprises continued when on the horizon there appeared two dozen large Native canoes. At the sighting both the Mi'kmaq and the accompanying *Rameurs* began a cheerful rhythmic chant: *"Owhaha, owhatha, owhatha."* Four handsome new outfits were then fitted on the "captives."

"These outfits are made from the wool cloth purchased from the Basques," Grandpa explained.

Nola couldn't help herself. "They're beautiful."

Dressed in full ceremonial regalia, Chief Toomy stepped onto one of the rafts and immediately called out to Hector, Jocelyne, Nola, and Frank in forceful Mi'kmaq, "Are you two couples ready to be wed?"

As this was translated by Grandpa, Jocelyne braced herself, holding on to Hector's hand. "I figured this might be what was happening."

Grandpa, standing next to the chief, repeated the question. "Are you two couples ready to wed?"

Joy, mixed with nervousness, led all four to blurt out an exultant "Yes, yes, yes, and yes!"

To the sound of drums, flutes, and castanets, Chief Toomy and Grandpa pronounced them man and wife.

"Kiss the bride!" several people cried.

And so it was done to great cheers and merriment. The two couples were raised onto the shoulders of several wedding party-goers and brought to two overturned voyageur canoes where an elaborate feast had been set out. Many pots and dishes were also placed on the rafts, and soon a full celebration was underway. With all the gaiety, few noticed when Zoopie and Zena managed to snatch several tasty morsels.

After a few hours of feasting, Chief Toomy called out, "Take the couples to the place we've prepared for them."

Each couple was escorted, six braves to a canoe, up the bay toward Whycocomagh. "Surely, they aren't taking us all the way back to their village," Frank whispered.

"I don't think so," Hector said. "That would take too long. But I can't think of where else they might be taking us."

The large canoes went so fast that less than four hours later, just as it was turning dark, they reached their destination. It was the little narrows quarry.

"Look at those two teepees!" Jocelyne cried. "They're awfully impressive."

"I love the festive drawings on them," Nola said.

The Native paddlers dropped off the two couples and left, indicating they would be back the next morning.

"Finally," Nola said, "some time with Frank without an escort. I love it! It's like we've been let out of jail!"

With great flourish and excitement, Frank lifted his bride and marched her off to the teepee, saying gleefully to Hector as he did so, "Bye, Hector."

The next morning, glowing with contentment and basking in the warmth of the early sunshine, Jocelyne and Nola insisted on preparing the breakfast the Mi'kmaq had left for them. All too soon, though, the voyageur canoes were back. And all too soon the two couples were on their return trip to Westmount.

"It's been too short," Jocelyne said. "I don't want this to end. Ever."

"That's true," Nola agreed, "but we've created memories we'll treasure forever."

Back at Westmount, the couples were met with another pleasant surprise. The *Rameurs* had started building each of the newlyweds their very own cabin. Hector was particularly pleased. "I was getting tired living cheek by jowl with a bunch of smelly young men. This new cabin's going to be a big improvement."

By the second anniversary of the refugees' flight from Grand Pré, many things were looking up at Westmount. The garden had produced bumper crops, the bees were producing record amounts of honey, the rabbit hutches were doing well, and many solid cabins had been constructed. Several of the residents had become skilled at reading, and a few, like Nola, had made great progress with writing. Provisions for defence were progressing. Sturdy embankments around most of the settlement were more than half completed, and a dozen fire pumps and four catapults had been built.

While relations with Louisbourg were stable, several fishing boats arriving at Westmount reported that they had to run a British blockade to get into the bay. French soldiers visiting Westmount confirmed that hostilities between Britain and France were getting worse.

Frank's distillation tower was producing adequate amounts of coal oil and charcoal for both trade and local consumption. "To me that tower is as beautiful as the most perfect church steeple," he told Hector one day. He felt that their supplies for defence were sufficient except for bleach production. "We have to focus our energies on producing more of those precious yellow grains. We only have fifteen barrels, and I'm sure that wouldn't be enough to stop an attack."

"What's the problem?" Hector asked. "You have more than ten men working on the project."

"Actually, I have only eight. Two of the French deserters left with the last Basque fishing boat. They said they'd bring back wives in the spring. Mostly, though, it's a matter of time. It's not easy to break up the red rock, and it takes a lot of coal to evaporate salt water."

"If I made you some more picks, chisels, and sledgehammers, would that help? I've found that if I plunge red-hot iron into cold water it hardens the metal."

"That would be great, Hector. Our chisels have gotten pretty dull. And could you make a grinding machine to crush the red rock, just like you did for the gypsum project? The boys are getting tired using sledgehammers to do the crushing. Do you have enough iron for that?"

"I can always use more iron, Frank. What we don't use ourselves the Mi'kmaq will always take. You know, we owe them a lot for that wonderful wedding party they put on for us."

"Yes, I'm sure, but we need a grinder, Hector. That should be our priority. Anyway, right now I've got to check if we finally arrived at the best bleach-coal oil proportion. I have a test batch out on that raft now. Let's get that young Sammy to shoot a flaming arrow at it to see how well it explodes. He'd love doing that."

"I'll go get him," Hector said.

Frank and Hector, not to say Nola and Jocelyne, vied with one another to make theirs the most stylish cabin. Although they all expressed doubts about this competition, none knew how to bring it to an end.

Nola expressed her frustration to Jocelyne. "Frank and I are being silly. Frank is spending way too much time building chairs and tables. There's no way he can do as good a job as your Hector. And I don't have your skill at sewing."

"Yes, Nola, but your paintings are much better than any I've ever drawn."

"I guess a little friendly competition doesn't hurt," Nola said.

"Actually," Frank complained when he heard this, "it's hurting something important — our production of bleach. We only have thirty barrels in stock. That's not enough to defend ourselves."

"In that case, I'm going to stop this foolish competition," Nola said. "Jocelyne and Hector are our friends, not competitors. Why don't you and Hector work together on improving the catapults? That should tone down the competition. Jocelyne and I can help."

Frank grinned. "That's a sensible solution, Nola."

8
War

In early May, Governor Drucour sent a courier to warn the Westmount residents: a British attack was imminent. Everybody was upset, but Frank was by far the most agitated.

"Hector, we've got to keep an eye on what's happening at Louisbourg," he said. "Some sort of relay should be organized so we can monitor what's going on. And we've got to make more of that bleach."

Hector frowned. "I'm with you on that relay idea, but surely the forty barrels of bleach we have is enough. It's Louisbourg that they'll attack, not us."

"If they attack Louisbourg, they'll come here, too. I've read military histories, and it's the rare battle that involves just one target. We have to get more of us to work on the bleach project."

Hector agreed to set up the relay. At the end of May this new route produced encouraging news. Joseph reported that French warships had anchored in front of the fortress. "The French fleet is impressive," he told them. "There are ten huge ships at anchor. I was told that the fleet has 494 guns and 3,870 battle-hardened men. There was supposed to be ten more ships, but these were turned away by the British blockade. Unfortunately, one of those turned away was the largest — the eighty-gun *Le Formidable*."

"It's comforting to hear that so much armaments and men have come to defend us," Grandpa said. "Too bad the others couldn't get through. There were almost twice as many French warships here last year. It looks like the British blockade is getting tighter."

The next report by Joseph was chillingly bad. On June 3 an immense British fleet anchored in Gabarus Bay, a scant six miles from the fortress. "The size of their fleet is shocking," Joseph told them. "I counted over a hundred ships at Gabarus, several larger than those in the French fleet. I'm sure they have thousands of more guns and many more men than the French."

"Then we're in deep, deep trouble," Frank said.

Nola asked Frank what he thought would happen.

"It's simple, Nola. Louisbourg will fall, then we'll be attacked and probably killed."

Hector heard this. "Don't be so gloomy, Frank. The fortress has mighty defences. They can handle the British, even if the odds are against them."

"I hope so, but I'm doubtful. It's clear the British have prepared well, and they're like bulldogs. Once they start a fight, they won't stop until they've won. They have much more firepower than the French, at least a four-to-one advantage if Joseph's report is correct."

Westmount was, unfortunately, not long in waiting for an attack. On June 11 the residents were stunned to see a large warship sail into their bay. Hector pulled out his spyglass. "It's flying the Union Jack! I see the name now. It's the *Shannon*. It looks like she has twenty-eight guns. They're coming after us!"

Frank ran to the shore, yelling, "I didn't expect them to attack so soon! Come on, men, get our catapults and fire pumps ready. Make sure they don't see anyone over our embankments. We want them to think we're totally defenceless."

Nola noticed that Hector scowled as Frank's tense voice resonated along the shoreline, but in the midst of nerve-wracking battle preparations, no one drew attention to Frank's single-minded, almost scary resolve. The warship anchored only a hundred yards from the little settlement's embankments.

"Arm those catapults and fill up the pumps!" Frank cried. "Then be absolutely quiet. Not a peep. And wait until my signal. I want them very close before we show our hand."

The *Rameurs* watched fearfully as they saw the *Shannon* launch twenty longboats. Each was manned with ten soldiers and loaded with muskets. Huddled behind the embankments, Frank signalled that they should allow the lead vessels to approach within ten yards. Hector fidgeted noticeably at this risky plan but kept his silence. This encounter was much worse than the skirmish with Governor Drucour.

As the boats came closer and Hector was almost bursting with impatience, Frank ordered, "*Now!* Spray them with all the fire we've got!"

Liquid fire leaped from the pumps, splashing each boat with sheets of flame. The attackers, astonishment pasted on their faces and desperate to douse their burning clothes, dived into the sea. This vaulting tipped several craft to their gunnels, causing many to capsize. Realizing their peril in further advance, the more distant boats reversed course and narrowly averted the next wave of *Rameur* flames.

At this development Frank snapped out two orders. "Drag those soldiers in the water ashore and secure their boats. The rest of you launch all catapults. I want that ship hit *hard*!"

Not one of the first salvo of bleach bombs hit the *Shannon*. Three overshot and one fell just short of the ship. Frank was furious. Glancing at Hector, he glared. "I knew we should have practised more. Adjust the lever up one notch on the first three and down one on the fourth. Launch again as soon as you've made the adjustments."

Before they could fire again, the *Shannon* blasted a broadside at the settlement. Several cabins were smashed to bits, killing the few who had foolishly stayed in them. The second *Rameur* salvo proved more successful: two direct hits cracked the *Shannon*'s main mast.

"Excellent!" Frank cried. "Keep firing!" He ordered his men to drag the drenched British oarsmen ashore. Then he told them to take off their jackets and blindfold them by wrapping the jackets around their heads.

All four barrels of the third salvo hit the ship, knocking out its quarterdeck and its second mast and setting all its sails ablaze. This punishment didn't stop the warship from firing its cannons again and again, but each time its aim became less accurate.

When the ten fleeing longboats reached the *Shannon*, tow lines were thrown to the oarsmen and anchor lines were cut. They began to row the crippled warship out of harm's way.

"They're getting away!" Frank shouted. "Keep launching those barrels!"

The *Rameurs* managed to launch another four salvos before the rowers succeeded in pulling the ship out of range. The *Shannon*'s main deck had suffered extensive damage. Few men on it could have escaped injury. But the ship itself carried on.

The whole incident — from appearance to departure of the ship — lasted less than three-quarters of an hour. Ninety longboat men had been captured; ten had drowned. Eight longboats were recovered, including their contents of muskets, a quantity of ammunition, and two Union Jacks. Five *Rameurs* lay dead.

The prisoners were treated for burns, were fed codfish chowder, and were marched off to work in the coal mine. As they marched past Nola, she recognized one prisoner as a soldier she had encountered at Grand Pré. She slapped him hard. "I remember you grabbing and pinching me. You're a beast!"

The man recoiled in dread.

Frank came up and asked, "What's going on here?"

"This animal groped me when we were at Grand Pré."

Anger flickered in Frank. "Well, the shoe's on the other foot now, isn't it, soldier? This lady is my wife. What do you think we should do with you and your bad behaviour?"

The soldier apologized, profusely begging Nola for forgiveness. Gracious in victory, she pledged the man to be more respectful of women and, that done, accepted his apology and sent him off to work.

Hector was delighted with the victory but miserable with his miscalculation. He had to accept that he had been wrong about the threat to Westmount. "What can I say, Frank, you were right."

Frank didn't answer directly, but shifted attention to immediate concerns. "We only have ten bomb barrels left after repelling that attack. We have to put those prisoners to work rebuilding our supplies."

"You make the decisions about our defence, Frank," Hector said. "It's obvious you know more about this than I do. If we'd followed my advice, we'd probably be captives of the British by now or dead. Without your discovery of how to make bleach bombs ... well, I don't want to even think about it."

"You're a good man, Hector. There's no need to put yourself down. We couldn't have done what we did without you."

That evening Frank confided in Nola about their prospects. "I don't want to scare people more than they are already, but I have little doubt that Louisbourg is doomed. I've talked to some of the prisoners, and it's clear they mean to crush the French. As soon as they're done at Louisbourg we'll be next."

"You aren't going to give up, are you?"

"Of course not. Hector agrees that I'm now the leader. I mean for us to fight until we win. Or die. Do you think the *Rameurs* are tough enough? Five of those who stayed in their cabins died and several were injured."

"We've already been through a lot, but everyone I've talked to is ready to fight. They know what it is to be a prisoner, and none want a life of subservience. I'm positive all will do what needs to be done."

"That's just what I wanted to hear," Frank said, hugging her gently. "It's certain that we'll have to work hard, but that, unfortunately, might not be enough."

Frank organized the prisoners into work gangs. "We'll operate in three shifts — one on the job, another getting food, and the last on break. Hector, we need to arrange guards for each of these shifts."

"I'll do that. How do you want the prisoners distributed among the coal mine, the distillation works, the red rock quarry, and the evaporation flats?"

"Our efforts must be focused on bleach production. Those yellow grains are the key to our defence. We have maybe a month before they attack again. We must have lots of bleach ready by then or it will be all over for us."

A week after repelling the *Shannon* the community experienced a heart-wrenching setback. Joseph went missing while on reconnaissance at Louisbourg. Hector reported to Frank, "He must have been captured or maybe killed."

Frank discovered that there had been only three men on relay duty. "That's not enough. I imagine Joseph was tired from all the travel and was spotted taking a rest. After all, it's thirty miles by land to Louisbourg."

Frank decided a rotating team of seven — one every five miles plus a spare ready to go — would be needed and that each would be armed with a musket. Because he wanted all available men for guard or bleach production jobs, he gave Jocelyne the responsibility for this task. "Do you have enough girls to handle this relay, Jocelyne?" he asked. "I don't have to tell you it's dangerous."

"I'll need to have them do some training first, but other than that I'm sure we can do it. We're eager to do our part."

Later, Nola asked Jocelyne why she had assigned little Adele to the relay team. "Adele has been pestering me for weeks to help," Jocelyne told her friend. "First, I was surprised by how well she learned to handle a musket and then she showed me the skills she'd picked up from our Mi'kmaq friends. She can camouflage herself so well and walk so noiselessly in the forest that she can almost fade out of sight magically. Adele is so good at these hunting skills that I despair she'll ever learn to become a proper young lady."

Two weeks later there was a positive, though bittersweet, interlude to the community's defence efforts. A Basque fishing boat carrying the two Louisbourg deserters and their new wives dropped anchor. The captain mentioned he had to travel to Westmount at night to avoid British patrols but that he was used to such manoeuvres and it had posed little real inconvenience. The arrival of the immigrants, plus the regular exchange of goods, gave a much-needed boost to everyone's spirits.

Frank was particularly pleased that the ship had brought a mercury thermometer. "I've wanted this for a long time. I'm going to put it to immediate use to check some temperatures on the distillation tower."

For a full month Jocelyne's team reported that the fortress defenders were holding out against the thousands of bombs and cannonballs hurled at them. Then, in mid-July, she reported that the defences were starting to crumble. The King's Bastion and almost all the larger structures in the fortress had been destroyed. "I'm sure they can't hold out much longer," she told Frank.

Although distraught, Frank wasn't surprised at this news. Production at the bleach works was progressing well. But who knew if it would be enough?

Frank learned from an officer prisoner that his uncle was one of the commanders of the force attacking Louisbourg. The overall commanders were General Amherst and Admiral Boscawen, but next in charge were Brigadiers Lawrence, Wolfe, and Whitmore. Frank mentioned this to Hector without comment, but secretly he hoped it could somehow be used to his advantage.

The last week of July Jocelyne reported Louisbourg had fallen. "I went myself and climbed a tree about half a mile from the fortress. I saw the British parade in and raise the Union Jack. There was utter misery in the faces of the defenders. Stacks and stacks of dead were heaped against the walls. It was a pitiful sight. The British have won." She began to sob inconsolably.

Frank understood what he had to do. He realized it wasn't wise to provoke the British lion unnecessarily, so he assembled the prisoners in the settlement's main square and stepped up on an overturned bucket to gain height. When Frank announced that Louisbourg had fallen, they cheered so passionately that it was a full five minutes before he could speak again. Then he told them the *Rameurs* were prepared to set them free as long as they pledged not to come back and attack the settlement.

This condition on their release gave rise to animated discussions among the prisoners. Eventually, the senior officer present raised his voice, responding for all. "We agree to your terms. We men of the *Shannon* will tell General Amherst we were released on the condition that we not come back to fight you."

As they were leaving, Frank told Hector, "I made sure their senior officer knew about my relationship to Brigadier Lawrence."

Ten days later guards observed what they had hoped they would never see again. On the horizon more than five hundred British troops in bright crimson were advancing on the settlement. Frank responded by raising one of their Union Jacks coupled with a green parley flag below it. At these signals the column of troops stopped. They were still one hundred and fifty yards from the embankment. After twenty minutes of no further movement, the *Rameurs* noticed one of the soldiers waving a green flag.

"They're accepting our parley!" Frank cried. "Hector, round up a guard of twenty armed men. Nola, I want you to come with me. We're going in front of the guard to a point halfway between us and that army."

The *Rameur* parley group, in passable military formation but makeshift attire, walked to the midpoint. A similar British group, crisply uniformed in fine crimson, soon broke from their ranks and marched in tight formation to the meeting point.

Recognizing his uncle, Frank initiated the negotiations. "Welcome to Westmount, Brigadier Lawrence."

The brigadier responded magnanimously. "I see you've raised the Union Jack, Frank. We finally have those scalawags under British authority. Well done, young man!"

Frank almost gasped at his uncle's callousness, but his voice remained calm. "We accept your authority in all our external relationships, but we reserve the right to set the rules for our own community. And as for calling these people scalawags, I'd like to introduce you to my wife, Nola."

Nola stepped forward, curtsied, and said in pleasantly accented English, "That's a formidable army you have, Brigadier Lawrence. Congratulations. But please understand that I am *not* a scalawag. I can read and write in two languages, and I can draw and paint. And I don't appreciate being called by that name." She stepped back.

Lawrence turned to look coldly at his nephew. "I see. May I ask what Anglican minister performed your marriage to this person, Frank?"

"Nola isn't an Anglican. She was brought up in the Catholic faith. In the absence of a regular priest, we were married by Chief Toomy, who is the properly constituted religious authority of the Mi'kmaq people."

"Ah, good, then in the eyes of the law you aren't married at all. You can still redeem yourself, young man. Come back to your people. Your father's been worried about you."

Furious but controlling his temper, Frank returned doggedly to the main issue. "We pledge to give no support to Britain's enemies. There should be no problem in allowing us to manage our own affairs."

"That isn't our standard arrangement with our colonies, young man. Why should yours be a special case?"

"We're ready as British subjects to contribute to the larger society. We produce valuable goods and are competent to run our settlement. We'll even sign a loyalty oath."

Not hiding his disdain, Lawrence pursed his lips. "You'll either surrender or you'll be wiped out. There can be no halfway status in such basic matters."

Frank continued resolutely. "We're ready and willing to be proper British subjects, but our property rights must be respected. We won't stand by idly and be ill treated as happened at Grand Pré."

Visibly angry, the brigadier signalled his guard that the meeting was over. "You may think you were clever with that little skirmish you had with the *Shannon*, but now you'll be dealing with the British Army. Your father would be very disappointed with you, Frank. Goodbye."

Frank bristled. "On the contrary, sir, I believe my father would be disappointed with your narrow and pig-headed attitude. Your actions aren't a credit to Britain."

Upset but unwavering in the rightness of their cause, Frank began the return to their defensive lines. On the way he said in a flat voice, "It's a real pity, but we a have a fight on our hands. Hector, move our catapults at the beach to the embankment facing the soldiers. There's no one attacking the beach. We must prove to them we know how to defend ourselves."

As they reached the embankment, Nola tugged on his sleeve. "We escaped their clutches at Grand Pré. We stopped the *Shannon*. We can stop them again."

Lawrence's assault started with hideously real cannonballs slamming into the entrenchments. They struck in so deeply that the whole structure shook. This fusillade was followed by a formation of highly disciplined soldiers advancing purposefully and firing their muskets at every tenth step.

Huddled behind their protective embankment and trenches, the *Rameurs* readied a dozen catapults and ten fire pumps. Frank waited until the first line of soldiers reached the seventy-five-yard mark. Then he gave the order: "Launch all catapults and reload immediately!"

Twelve bleach bombs arced across the sky and burst in mighty blasts right at the seventy-five-yard line, sending the confident formation into jagged disarray. The noise from these blasts had barely died down when the second line stepped over those stricken by the first salvo. These men were hit with another volley of bombs that detonated with the same deadly effect. Relentless in their attack, a third line of troops stepped into the breach.

"Reload, men, but hold your fire," Frank ordered. "Let's see what they do. I hope our salvoes have shaken their confidence."

It wasn't to be, though. The third line marched toward the embankments, less numerous but as determined as the first two.

"They aren't letting our punishment stop them," Frank said. "They're tough, but so are we!"

At the fifteen-yard mark Frank ordered their fire pumps into action, supported by a full volley of catapult bombs. This brutal pounding pummelled the British troops so viciously that the advance hobbled to a stop. Those that could began a helter-skelter retreat.

Hector observed the battlefield with sadness. "They've suffered a high number of casualties. There must be over fifty men writhing on the ground out there."

"They'll pick them up," Frank said. "That's a sad ritual of war."

Over the next hour the *Rameurs* watched as the British picked up their wounded and dead. Then, by late afternoon, they saw the troops slowly move back toward Louisbourg.

"It's not over yet," Frank said ruefully. "My uncle's nothing if not tenacious. I'm sure they'll be back. And next time they'll have even more soldiers and cannons. We must work all out to be ready."

After all the carnage of battle, the *Rameurs* were numb with a mixture of relief and grief. Several cabins had been destroyed, and many defenders had suffered injury, though most were comparatively minor. All regarded the wounds as badges of honour.

The precious distillation tower and evaporation works were only slightly damaged, so Frank immediately ordered an intense effort to rebuild their stock of bleach bombs. "I don't know how much time before the next assault, but we have to make the best use of any lull we have."

That evening he confided to Nola. "I understand more about Britain now that I've fought against their army. My uncle's an obstinate man focused only on conquest. He has a vicious streak that seems to prevent him from ruling intelligently. He's mistrustful of anyone who doesn't fit his narrow view of things. My father isn't like that. I'm sure he would favour our stand here."

"You hate seeing the strong oppress the weak, Frank." Giving him a peck on the cheek, Nola added, "That's one of the many reasons I married you."

Preparation for the coming assault meant, Frank decided, more catapults had to be constructed. "We need at least twenty-five to defend all our embankments, plus another ten fire pumps. And we have to cut some trees and throw them into the trenches to make it more of an obstacle course."

Everyone started work with an eagerness that gladdened Frank's heart. He made sure this work was well underway before turning his attention to the bleach supply. Frank decided they could stretch supplies by using ordinary coal oil barrels to make up for shortfalls. "We can spike them with lime and charcoal," he said. "That will extend our supplies yet still make a fair weapon. There won't be an explosion, but a good amount of raw fire will confuse the attackers."

Some of the younger boys and girls approached Frank, curious about the many explosions they had seen. "Could you tell us what makes those blasts?" Remy asked.

"I'm glad to see such curiosity, young man. That's the way I learn myself. I'm interested in what things are made of, so I do a set of tests to find out. For example, did you know when you burn lime it has a red colour and that when you burn sea salt it burns with a blue flame?"

"No," Adele said, "I didn't know that."

"Well, it does. Then some materials contain more hidden energy than others. You can think of it as a ladder of heat with some materials, like our yellow grains, containing more internal heat than others like, say, gypsum. When we combine two high-heat energy compounds, we can make a third material that's even more powerful. It has more hidden energy than the original materials. That's the process, a sort of heat ladder, by which bleach bombs are made."

"You make it sound easy," Remy said. "Those bombs are really scary, though."

"You know that thermometer I just got from the Basques? I use it to separate liquids according to their rate of evaporation. Those that evaporate more easily come off first. These high-volatile liquids burn faster than heavier liquids, and we use them in the fire barrels we're preparing."

He sent the youngsters back to work with the comment: "Even when an experiment doesn't work out as expected, that doesn't mean it was a failure. It can point you to something else. Bit by bit, you build up your knowledge, and if you're persistent, keep careful notes, and think about what you're doing, then eventually you'll succeed."

Only twelve days after Brigadier Lawrence's army had withdrawn, a second assault group came over the horizon, just as Frank had predicted. Hector viewed the advancing columns with great sorrow. "There must be fifteen hundred of them out there and lots of cannons."

"That's a truly dreadful sight," Frank agreed. "They mean to wipe us out. To my uncle anybody who doesn't submit must die. He's brutal."

"Perhaps so," Nola said. "But let's not forget that your uncle isn't invincible."

"That's true," Frank said. "This time, however, I'm sure we're going to have a fight to the death. It's already late in the afternoon, so they might delay the attack until morning."

To Frank's surprise, Lawrence didn't wait. As soon as his troops pulled into range, a fierce cannonade hit the *Rameurs*. It was so blistering that within fifteen minutes nothing was left of Westmount's cabins but rubble. Frank's precious distillation tower, along with every other built-up structure, had been smashed to bits.

The dust from this barrage was still in the air when they saw the first line of soldiers form. It was a full one hundred yards across. "That line is twice as wide as the first attack," Frank said. "It's a good thing we built those extra catapults and fire pumps. We'll let them advance to the seventy-five-yard mark before launching our bombs."

When the first troops reached the mark set by Frank, all twenty-five catapults launched their deadly loads. These exploded with tremendous blasts. Hector noticed that Lawrence had equipped each soldier with a fire-dowsing cape designed to provide protection. However, the capes did little to stop the flames. "I'm sure the brigadier's very disappointed that his new capes didn't help much," Hector mused.

Rigorous discipline — developed over long months of training — impelled the second line to step past those stricken by the first *Rameur* volley. The catapults fired again. The attackers faltered once more, and fewer soldiers managed to pick themselves up to press on toward the embankments. Despite the fierce pummelling, the third line filled breaches in the ranks and steadfastly continued on to the forty-yard mark still in fair formation. Then a combined bleach bomb/fire volley — everything in the *Rameur* arsenal — slammed into the British.

Frank shouted orders for the catapults to reload immediately and for the fire pumps to again spray their lethal loads. These assaults punched huge holes in the attacking phalanx. Yet after much wobbling, more than two hundred troops, their faces grimly determined, charged onward, bellowing fierce battle cries as they did so.

The *Rameur* back defences flung fire grenades at these two hundred as they attempted to straddle the tree-strewn trenches. They managed to stop all except for twenty. These fierce few bounded through the explosions seemingly unscathed and climbed over the embankment. A vicious musket/bayonet onslaught began to batter at the *Rameur* main defence corps.

Observing this melee from less than thirty feet away, Jocelyne realized she had no choice. She and her team threw several grapefruit-sized bleach bombs directly into the centre of the killing frenzy. The explosions knocked down all the combatants in the blast area. These staunched the breach, allowing the defenders to rally and seal the gap in the *Rameur* line.

Wounded soldiers started to retreat from this wall of fire. His jaw clenched, Frank ordered a further volley of barrels. "We don't want them to dally."

The battlefield left by the attackers was strewn with bodies and pitiful moaning. In the distance, Frank observed three British commanders scanning the field with their spyglasses. "I hope this carnage will give them pause before they launch another assault," he muttered to himself. "We've all suffered enough."

A distraught Nola, attempting to comfort a trembling Zoopie, sobbed. "Grandpa was killed in that last attack, Frank. He was stabbed in the chest by a bayonet. It's horrible!"

Jocelyne moaned. "Those grenades my team threw killed many of our own people."

Hector attempted to console her. "If you hadn't done that, we'd all be dead. You had to throw them."

Dusk was already upon the field when the British troops began the pickup of their dead and wounded.

Frank checked what supplies they had left and then called a war council. "We can't survive another assault. We don't have enough ammunition and we've already lost twenty of our own. There's only one way to stop them. We have to launch a raid as soon as it's dark to blow up their stores of gunpowder."

"That's a pretty difficult assignment, Frank," Hector said.

"It's tough, but it's the only way. I know from talking to the *Shannon* prisoners how the British Army operates. They normally have a few supply wagons about two thousand yards back of the front lines. We have to find those wagons with the gunpowder and blow them up. I think they'd have sent more troops to fight us if they had more gunpowder, so they must be quite short. Their assault on Louisbourg must have taken most of the supplies they had. We have to hit them hard where they're most vulnerable."

Nola kissed Frank gently on the cheek. "I'm glad you're in charge of our defence, dear. Without you we'd be finished for sure."

Frank smiled thinly, then went on to explain that he needed twenty men for the assignment — four to carry a catapult, eight to carry bomb barrels, and eight to provide musket cover. He didn't need to emphasize how dangerous the assignment was. But when he asked for volunteers, he was delighted to see so many were ready to serve.

"You're a brave bunch," he said, deeply moved.

Shortly after midnight, the raiding party set out over the embankment, moving as quickly and quietly as possible. They headed five hundred yards away from the main encampment, crouching and zigzagging over the terrain to check for wagons. Frank had taken Hector's spyglass, since he knew best what to look for. Every couple of hundred yards they stopped and scouted around as well as they could in the dim moonlight. At the third stop Frank, seeing a guard glancing in their direction, gestured for an immediate crouch down. When they reached the two-thousand-yard range with no luck, Frank had the men crawl back toward their encampment.

Finally, they spotted the wagons they were looking for three-quarters of an hour into the mission. Frank was certain he had the right wagons now, so he motioned for the catapult team to get ready. Then he gave the go-ahead.

The first bomb hit a wagon, but there was no secondary explosion, so Frank had his men reposition to strike the second target. This volley caused a huge double explosion. "Pay dirt!" Frank whooped. The third bomb fell short, but the last one scored again, and a huge explosion ruptured the darkened skyline.

To a rising crescendo of shouts, the raiders dumped their catapult and raced back the way they had come. Hundreds of musket shots whizzed over their heads. They were within sight of the embankments when several

British troops moved to cut off their escape. *Rameur* musket shots rang out, and the English soldiers dodged away. Only fifty yards from safety, Frank and his companions were again caught, and this time several shots felled five of the raiders. Three of these were obviously dead; Hector and Frank were shot but still mobile, barely. Firing as best they could, the remaining *Rameurs* cleared a narrow pathway of tree obstacles and dragged themselves to the embankments where several defenders helped pull them over.

While volleys of *Rameur* shots forced the attackers to retreat, Nola and Jocelyne grabbed their husbands, tore open the clothing covering their wounds, and did their utmost to stop the bleeding. Others brought over clean rags to wash the dirt embedded in the gashes. This operation was so painful that both young men lost consciousness.

They awoke as dawn touched the horizon to perceive dimly the worried faces of their wives. Shot in the leg, Frank smiled feebly and asked, "Did you force them back?" Then, suddenly anxious, he added, "Am going to live?"

Before anyone could answer, Hector growled, "They got my other leg this time. Those British really have it in for me."

Nola and Jocelyne reacted in unison "Thank God, you're alive!"

The morning light brought a hopeful development. The British, it seemed, were preparing to depart. Told of this, Frank said, grimacing with pain and fatigue, "I knew that after the siege of Louisbourg they'd be short of gunpowder. If they really are leaving, then I guess our raid paid off."

With a combination of pride and gratitude, Nola said, "That was a daring manoeuvre, Frank, but we're very fortunate they're going. If they knew we were out of bombs, they'd surely strike us again." Then, lifted by a wave of emotion as she gazed at the line of departing soldiers, she added, "We don't know if they'll be back next year or the year after, but for now at least we're survivors. We have our homes again, such as they are after that horrible bombardment. We've had more than enough of people who want to do us harm."

Nola studied the dew sparkling on the grass and felt as if everything had been washed clean by the battle. "Louisbourg has fallen, French power in Cape Breton is finished, and the British have won their main objective. They don't need to attack us anymore. After all, we fly the Union Jack. It must have seemed strange for them to be attacking a town flying their own flag. We have, I think, a good chance to be left in peace."

Selected Reading
and Websites

Books

Brumwell, Stephen. *Paths of Glory: The Life and Death of General James Wolfe*. Montreal: McGill-Queen's University Press, 2008.

Chartrand, René. *Louisbourg 1758: Wolfe's First Siege*. Oxford, Eng: Osprey Publishing, 2000.

CRC Handbook of Chemistry and Physics. Student edition. Boca Raton, FL: CRC Press, 1988.

Cross, Michael S., and Gregory S. Kealey. *Economy and Society During the French Regime, to 1759.* Toronto: McClelland & Stewart, 1983.

Davison, Marion. *Smoke over Grand Pré.* St. John's: Breakwater Books, 2004.

Doucet, Clive. *Notes from Exile: On Being Acadian.* Toronto: McClelland & Stewart, 2000.

____. *Lost and Found in Acadie.* Halifax: Nimbus Publishing, 2004.

Fowler, William. *Empires at War: Seven Years' War and the Struggle for North America.* Vancouver: Douglas & McIntyre, 2005.

Jobb, Dean W. *The Acadians: A People's Story of Exile and Triumph.* Toronto: John Wiley & Sons, 2005.

Johnston, A.J.B. *Endgame 1758: The Promise, the Glory, and the Despair of Louisbourg's Last Decade.* Lincoln, NE: University of Nebraska Press, 2008.

Laxer, James. *The Acadians: In Search of a Homeland*. Toronto: Anchor Canada, 2007.

MacLeod, D.P. *Northern Armageddon: The Battle of the Plains of Abraham, Eight Minutes of Gunfire That Shaped a Continent*. Vancouver: Douglas & McIntyre, 2008.

Marston, Daniel. *The Seven Years' War*. Oxford, Eng: Osprey Publishing, 2001.

Moore, Christopher. *Louisbourg Portraits: Five Dramatic, True Tales of People Who Lived in an Eighteenth-Century Garrison Town*. Toronto: McClelland & Stewart, 2000.

Shreve, Randolph Norris. *Shreve's Chemical Process Industries*. Ed. G.T. Austin. 5th ed. New York: McGraw-Hill, 1984.

Stecher, Paul G., ed. *Merck Index: An Encyclopedia of Chemicals and Drugs*. 8th ed. Rathway, NJ: Merck, 1968.

John Skelton

Trottier, Maxine. *Dear Canada: Death of My Country: The Plains of Abraham Diary of Geneviève Aubuchon.* Toronto: Scholastic Canada, 2005.

Websites

Acadians: *www.cbc.ca/acadian.* Discover the amazing history of Acadians with this site, featuring timelines, interactive maps, and additional resources.

Grand Pré: *www.grand-pre.com.* Plan a trip with this guide to Grand Pré, which covers its incredible history, events, and must-see attractions.

James Wolfe: *www.militaryheritage.com/wolfe.htm.* This biography of General James Wolfe gives a thrilling account of his time fighting in the Seven Years' War.

Louisbourg: *www.louisbourg.ca/fort.* Relive the past with this detailed account of life in Louisbourg during the Seven Years' War.

Nova Scotia: *www.novascotia.com.* This site contains extensive accounts of Nova Scotia, including information on Acadians and the Seven Years' War.

Plains of Abraham: *www.ccbn-nbc.gc.ca/_en/index.php*. Explore the past, present, and future of this historical park through descriptions of important battles, current sights, and future events.

Science in *Band of Acadians*: *www.bandofacadians.ca*. Site provides information and links on the geology and chemical reactions cited in the novel.

Seven Years' War: *www.thecanadianencyclopedia.com/index.cfm?PgNm=TCE&Params=a1ARTA0007300*. A complete and informative history of the Seven Years' War and North American participation in it.

Shallops: *www.mit.edu/people/bpfoley/shallop.html*. This site describes the seventeenth-century vessels and their uses with accompanying photographs.

MORE GREAT FICTION FOR YOUNG PEOPLE

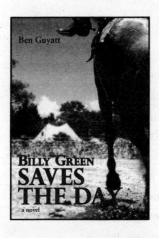

Billy Green Saves the Day
by Ben Guyatt
$12.99
978-1-55488-041-6

Eighteen-year-old Billy Green is an expert woodsman with romantic ideas of combat. But when the War of 1812 breaks out between the British in Canada and the United States, Billy finds himself faced with a series of fateful decisions. On June 5, 1813, he spots the massive American forces camped in the tiny hamlet of Stoney Creek. Can Billy help save the day for Canada?

Laughing Wolf
by Nicholas Maes
978-1-55488-385-1
$12.99

When a mysterious plague breaks out in the year
2213 and puts humanity on the brink of eradication,
fifteen-year-old Felix Taylor, the last healthy person
on Earth who can speak and read Latin, must project
back in time to ancient Rome and the era of Sparta-
cus to retrieve the only possible cure, a flower called
Laughing Wolf that has been extinct for more than
two thousand years.

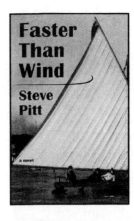

Faster Than Wind
by Steve Pitt
$11.99
978-1-55002-837-9

It is 1906, and fifteen-year-old newspaper boy and avid iceboat racer Bertie McCross fights to keep out of the clutches of the Kelly Gang, a family of slightly older Toronto toughs who are shaking down "newsies." The continued pursuit by the Kelly Gang, a plunge into freezing harbour water, and the clash of classes all lead up to a spine-tingling race to end all races.

Available at your favourite bookseller.

DUNDURN PRESS
w w w . d u n d u r n . c o m

**Tell us your story!
What did you think of this book?**

Join the conversation at
www.definingcanada.ca/tell-your-story
by telling us what you think.